ELIZABELLA

Meets Her Match

Zoë Norton Lodge

* with illustrations by *

Georgia Norton Lodge

D1392169

First published in Great Britain 2019 by Walker Books Ltd
87 Vauxhall Walk, London SE11 5HJ

2 4 6 8 10 9 7 5 3 1

Text © 2018 Zoë Norton Lodge
Illustrations © 2018 Georgia Norton Lodge

The right of Zoë Norton Lodge and Georgia Norton Lodge
to be identified as author and illustrator respectively
of this work has been asserted by them in accordance
with the Copyright, Designs and Patents Act 1988

This book has been typeset in Vernonan Light Educational

Printed and bound by CPI Group (UK) Ltd, Croydon CR0 4YY

British Library Cataloguing in Publication Data:
a catalogue record for this book is available from the British Library

ISBN 978-1-4063-8906-7

www.walker.co.uk

For Rufus

Chapter One

Roses are red
Violets are blue
Sorry I was mean
IOU a haiku

Elizabella finished scribbling the poem on a sticky note. Every time she thought she might have upset someone, Elizabella would write a Sorry Poem to make amends. But this morning she had run out of time, having spent an awfully long while, even longer than usual, dealing with the giant knot in her hair.

While some people would spray some detangling conditioner and brush it out, Elizabella was quite proud of her knot. She would tease it with her fingers, making it grow a little bigger each day, like a science project.

Elizabella was ten and a quarter. She had brown hair and brown eyes and brown freckles on her cheeks. And even though she wasn't notably tall or short, she was always in the back row of school photos because her giant knot gave her bonus elevation.

This particular morning, Elizabella had spent so long working on her knot that she didn't have time to compose a proper Sorry Poem. She needed to write one for her brother, Toddberry, because the day before she had replaced the cheese sandwich in his lunch box with a picture of a cheese sandwich that she had drawn. Elizabella didn't get to see her brother discover it, because he was in Year Eight at Bilby Creek High School. But just the thought of him opening the box, pulling out the picture and staring at it completely confused made her laugh.

Even though she thought it was an excellent joke, when Toddberry had discovered an apple, a muesli bar, a tub of yogurt, a chocolate frog and a picture of a cheese sandwich in his lunch box, he was baffled and cross. So a Sorry Poem was in order. But it would have to wait.

She had some regrets about promising her brother a haiku, given she had no idea what a haiku was, but it was the only type of poem she had heard of that rhymed with "blue". **Being a writer is hard,** thought Elizabella as she stuck the placeholder poem to her brother's door.

"Bye, Toddberry!" she yelled. She wasn't planning on waiting for a reply, yet as she spoke, Toddberry emerge...

His hair was long and black and it tended to conceal most of his face. It was also full of knots, although they weren't intentional like Elizabella's. He had a habit of swishing his hair away to momentarily reveal his expression before the hair would fall back into place, covering him up, like curtains closing at the end of a play.

Toddberry swished his hair curtains and stared at his little sister. His expression: betrayal.

"I've left you a Sorry Poem," she said. "Well, a placeholder one, anyway."

"Can I *eat* it?" he asked pointedly.

"Ummm, sure," said Elizabella. "If you're a termite or a silverfish or a cockroach! See ya!"

She thundered down the hallway and flung open the front door, calling out goodbye to all the other humans and animals on her way out. "Bye, Dad! Bye, Larry! Bye, worms!"

Elizabella was excited to get to school. The sooner she got there, the sooner the term would end, and at the end of this term was the Bilby Creek Fête. She was opening the gate when her dad, Martin, ran out of the house behind her. He was very tall, with big, friendly, brown eyes like a labrador. He had dark, knotty hair too – knots ran in the family. He was holding her backpack, her lunch box, her homework, her recorder and her shoes. "Elizabella, you forgot your ... everything!"

Elizabella plonked herself down on the porch, while her dad put her shoes on for her and filled the backpack with all the things that had slipped her mind. "Thanks, Dad!"

He was just zipping up her backpack when Larry the Frillneck Lizard popped his head out of it.

"Larry, what are you doing in there?" Martin pulled him out, then he looked at Elizabella, one eye squinted.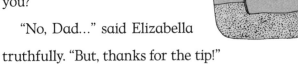

"You weren't going to take Larry to school for some Elizabella-type scheme, were you?"

"No, Dad..." said Elizabella truthfully. "But, thanks for the tip!"

Martin sighed. "Please don't get into any trouble today, my little entrepreneur, OK?"

"Dad, I will try my best."

"Promise?"

"I promise that there is a possibility that I won't get in trouble today."

Martin looked at her. He knew that was about the best he was going to get.

Elizabella shut the gate and started scuffing down the street. **She liked to really push her feet into the dirt as she walked,** kicking it up and coating her trainers and socks in a pleasing powdery layer of brown.

"Why did we give her that idea?" said Martin to Larry, as he waved goodbye to Elizabella.

"Don't ask me, that was all you," said Larry, in his native tongue Lizish, which to Martin sounded like meaningless croaks. Larry was completely versed in the English language; after all, he'd been listening to the whole family speak it his entire life. However, he hadn't worked out how to make his lizard mouth form the words correctly, so he was never really sure if anyone could understand him. It was incredibly frustrating.

Elizabella began walking to school, past all the little houses with their neatly trimmed bushes, freshly painted fences and shiny garden gnomes. Her house stood out in comparison. While it did have a flourishing lavender bush, the front garden of Elizabella's house was mostly adorned with old shoes and her unfinished household projects – half a homemade sundial, a pile of toilet rolls that may one day become a telescope of sorts, the old TV she was going to convert into a fish tank...

As Elizabella walked, she started thinking about all the things she could do if she brought Larry with her to Bilby Creek Primary School. She could put him in a teacher's drawer, in the drinking fountain, on a toilet seat, or maybe in Daphne's hair?

At the end of her street the houses disappeared and the path to school became wide and bushy. She was thinking so much that she didn't even realize she'd walked straight into a prickly acacia shrub.

"Elizabella, is that you?"

It was Huck. Huck had glasses and sandy blond hair and one pair of slime-green plimsolls that he wore every day even though one of the shoes had a big hole in it. Huck lived with his mum, Leanne, on the street parallel to Elizabella's. Their houses shared a back fence, so if they both stood in their gardens they could have a conversation.

Huck liked Elizabella because he never knew what she was going to do next. She eventually appeared out the other side of the shrub.

"Elizabella, you have prickles all over you!" said Huck. He began to pick them off her shirt.

"Don't throw them away!" said Elizabella.

"What could you want with them?"

"I have no idea, but definitely something." Elizabella started putting the prickles in her pocket.

Sometime later, Elizabella and Huck arrived at school. Bilby Creek Primary was a two-storey brick building that stood surrounded by trees and shrubs and bush. Because it had no neighbours, the school looked like a doll's house that belonged to a giant – a giant who had accidentally dropped her doll's house on the ground and left it outside to weather the elements.

Elizabella surveyed the empty school playground, pleased.

"Elizabella, nobody is here…"

"Oh, we must be really early!"

"No, Elizabella," said Huck nervously. "I think it's the opposite."

Elizabella glanced at her watch. It was 9.10 – the bell had gone ten minutes ago.

Mr Gobblefrump, the Acting Principal, walked purposefully towards them. He was obsessed with the rules. So much so that he wrote the Bilby Creek Primary School Rule Book and **did playground duty every day.** Mr Gobblefrump looked a bit like Humpty Dumpty with a toupee.

"Elizabella, do you know what the time is?"

"Why yes, Mr Gobblefrump, it's ten past nine."

"And what time does the bell go, Elizabella?"

"That would be o-nine-hundred hours, sir."

"And why are you late?"

"The thing is, I walked into a—"

Mr Gobblefrump stopped listening to her – he was distracted by Huck.

"Huck, why are you covered in –" Mr Gobblefrump pulled a prickle off Huck's shirt – "prickles!"

"Like I was saying," said Elizabella, "I walked into

a prickly acacia shrub and Huck was trying to help me pull off the prickles and when we were walking to school I started sticking them onto the back of his shirt in the shape of an 'H'." She spun Huck around. "See, 'H' for 'Huck'!"

"What?" said Huck, surprised. Such was Elizabella's sleight of hand, Huck had absolutely no idea any of this had occurred. He started running in little circles on the spot, trying to see his own back.

"Huck, go to the toilets and de-prickle yourself. And Elizabella, you must spend fifteen minutes in the Think About What You've Done Corner this morning. That's the rule."

"For putting prickles on shirts?" asked Elizabella.

"No," said Mr Gobblefrump, "for lateness." He briefly consulted the rule book, which he kept in his breast pocket. "Seems there is no prickle rule …

hmmm, I might need to update that for the next edition!"

In the toilets, Huck turned his back to the mirror and craned his neck around to see it. And sure enough, there in the middle of his back was a giant "H".

How did she do that without me noticing? thought Huck. *Very cool.*

★ ★ ★

Elizabella walked down the corridor with Mr Gobblefrump right on her tail.

"Sir, I can find my own way to class, you know," she said.

"If I don't escort you, who knows where you might end up?" he said. "In a frangipani tree, probably!"

Elizabella thought about this for a moment.

"Fair enough."

They were just about to reach her classroom, when Elizabella remembered something. "Can I ask you something, Mr Gobblefrump?"

Mr Gobblefrump sighed. "Yes...?"

"What's a haiku?"

Mr Gobblefrump stopped in his tracks. His yellowy moustache stood on end, sensing danger. This was the last thing he was expecting Elizabella to ask. He paused. *Could Elizabella possibly use the knowledge of what a haiku is to cause trouble?* He couldn't imagine how that might be.

"Well," he started, "a haiku is a Japanese poem, traditionally made up of seventeen syllables over three lines. The first line has five syllables, the next line has seven, and the final line has five. So it goes **Da-da-da-da-da**, then **da-da-da-da-da-da-da**, then another **da-da-da-da-da**."

"Does it rhyme?"

"It doesn't have to, though I suppose it could."

"Thanks," said Elizabella, entering her class. "Bye, sir!" She tried to close the door, but something was stopping her. She looked down and saw Mr Gobblefrump's big, blue plastic sandal jamming the door open like a giant squishy piece of LEGO.

"Not so fast," he said. "Miss Carrol?"

Miss Carrol taught Elizabella's Year Four class.

She had bright red hair and wore blouses tucked into high-waisted trousers almost every day.

She looked to the door. So did all of the children.

"Elizabella needs to spend fifteen minutes in the Think About What You've Done Corner," said Mr Gobblefrump.

Miss Carrol sighed. "OK, thank you."

Satisfied, Mr Gobblefrump left.

Elizabella went and sat there.

"Now, where were we?" said Miss Carrol, getting on with the lesson. "Ah, yes. What is eleven times six?"

Daphne's hand shot up. Daphne always wore her blonde hair in two little pigtails with pink baubles. Her eyes were the bluey-green of an emu's egg and she had a voice like a baby emu's to match.

"Yes, Daphne?"

Daphne scratched her head for a moment. Maths was her favourite subject and she often got so excited that she would put up her hand to answer the question before the answer had fully formed in her mind. Daphne started counting on her fingers. "Ummmm … ummmmm."

Elizabella couldn't stand it any more. "Sixty-six!" she blurted out.

"Sixty-six!" said Daphne immediately afterwards.

"Elizabella, no answering from the Think About What You've Done Corner, you know that. But … yes, you are right."

Daphne looked annoyed. She turned to Elizabella and stuck out her tongue.

"Sorry, Miss Carrol," said Elizabella. She decided to use the rest of her time in the corner working on her Sorry Poem for Toddberry.

Once in your lunch box
You had a nice cheese sandwich
I took it, my bad

Elizabella paused. *Wow,* she thought. *Haikus are easy.*

She tried another one:

I took your sandwich
Replaced it with a picture
My apologies

She was on a roll!

There was a picture
Instead of a cheese sandwich
Inside your lunch box

Elizabella thought, *That last one doesn't really have an apology in it.* She was just wondering how to rework it when Huck came into the room. A new haiku formed in her mind:

Huck, you're a cool dude.
Sorry about the prickles
Please don't think I'm rude

She paused. *Where did that come from?*

Chapter Two

It was breaktime and everyone was tumbling out and into their usual spots in the playground. Elizabella plopped down the stairs with her muesli bar and juice carton. *Ick,* she thought. *Lemony Pinch.* It was a net loss for the children at Bilby Creek Primary that the Bilby Creek Good Time Supermarket had a sale on Lemony Pinch, which everyone knows is the grossest juice flavour in the universe. It seemed like everybody's parents had taken advantage of the buy-in-bulk discount and had bought enough to last all the kids until the end of high school.

Elizabella sat down on the HOME segment of the hopscotch court, her regular seat. It was right next to one of the handball courts, which Elizabella and her friends usually played on during break and lunch. Handball was popular at Bilby Creek Primary and there were four handball courts, one in each corner of the playground.

Evie and Ava Price, the twins, were sitting down already. They were the shortest two kids in the class and their voices were the deepest. They had matching brown bobs, which they helpfully parted on opposite sides from each other (Evie's on the right, Ava's on the left) as a clue for people who struggled to tell them apart. It also meant they could easily pretend to be each other by parting their hair on the opposite sides when they wanted to confuse people. They each held a Lemony Pinch juice carton and were taking delicate, reluctant sips.

"It tastes like washing-up liquid," said Evie.

"It tastes like dog-food sauce," said Ava.

"It tastes like the dog licked up all the washing-up liquid and dog-food sauce in all of Bilby Creek then did the biggest wee in the world and all the parents collected the wee and fed it to their kids!" Evie continued.

"It tastes like tinned tuna sludge," Elizabella piped up, looking at her own juice carton, "and battery acid and old man snot!" She felt her passions rising. "It tastes like last week's milk mixed with the juices of a cat's kidney, dipped in the toilet after all the brothers in Bilby Creek used that toilet!"

"Puuuuke!" said Evie and Ava at the same time, as they sometimes did by accident.

"What are you guys talking about?" asked Huck, approaching the hopscotch court. Then he saw Ava and Evie retching. "Oh, Lemony Pinch. I chucked mine in the bin."

Elizabella suddenly had a fantastic idea. "Huck, go get me that juice carton!"

Huck thought about shoving his hand into the sticky juice-and-ant stew that lay at the bottom of the bin. He was about to ask Elizabella why she wanted him to do such a gross thing, but she had her Planning Face on. Sometimes it was better to just roll with Elizabella's schemes, so he shrugged and went over to rummage through the rubbish.

Elizabella had realized that there were probably hundreds of unopened Lemony Pinch juice cartons in the school bins. And while they may not be good for drinking, that didn't mean they couldn't be useful.

After all, what type of liquid does everyone love, even though it smells like wee?

Swimming pool liquid.

"Evie, Ava, go tell everyone to bring their sandwich cling film and unwanted Lemony Pinches to the sandpit," instructed Elizabella.

The twins went off and Elizabella set out on a surveying mission. The sandpit was tucked away behind the bike sheds where nobody ever went.

"Just as I thought," she said, approaching the tatty pit that was empty save for a few grotty clumps of sand, half a tennis ball and Gavin, who everyone called Sandy because he always seemed to have sand falling out of his pockets and shoes. Now Elizabella knew why. Sandy's mum shaved his head every week to prevent nits.

"This will be a perfect swimming pool," Elizabella declared.

Sandy looked at her. "A swimming pool?! That's heaps better than what I do here."

"What *do* you do here, Sandy?" asked Elizabella.

"Not a lot. I just want to make sure I'm first in when the sand comes back."

"You can be first in the pool," said Elizabella. Sandy beamed.

The kids started coming over with their cling film and Elizabella supervised as they placed piece after piece at the base of the sandpit, beginning its **transformation.**

Soon more kids were getting wind of the plan,

arriving with other items that could keep the bottom of the pool sealed – plastic bags, bin liners, raincoats.

Sandy came up to Elizabella, his arms full of big stones. "To weigh down the plastic when we fill up the pool," he explained. He put them on the ground, and pulled a glue stick out of his pocket. "And this is for leaks!"

"Genius," said Elizabella.

Sandy got to work strategically placing the stones around the base of the sandpit, where they would keep the plastic anchored to the ground.

Before long, it was looking sturdy. Huck had returned with dozens and dozens of kids, each of them armed with as many Lemony Pinches as they could carry.

"Fill her up?" asked Huck.

"Fill her up," said Elizabella, folding her arms with satisfaction.

And with that, everyone started gathering around the edge of the pit, squeezing carton after carton of the putrid substance onto the scrappy plastic base.

The juice level began to rise and rise.

Eventually, after what felt like ten minutes (because it was), the sandpit had been transformed.

Elizabella stood in front of it and commanded everybody's attention.

"Before I declare her officially open, there are some people I would like to thank. Yes, it may have been my idea, but it takes many brave and dedicated people to turn a tired, old sandpit into a beautiful swimming pool. This couldn't have happened without all of you who donated your plastic goods for her trusty base. Special mention to Sandy, who had the inspired idea of adding stones to make sure the plastic didn't rise to the top. A big thanks to Huck and his team for going through all the lunch boxes and all the bins to rescue all the Lemony Pinches. To all the collectors, all the assemblers and all the juice carton squeezers, thank you. And, of course, the biggest thanks of all goes to our parents. Thanks for being so stingy that you provided us with enough undrinkable liquid that we could literally make a pool!"

Huck sensed that the lengthy speech was coming

to an end, so he started to clap. Everybody followed suit.

"And now," continued Elizabella, turning to the creation, "I name you 'Pit Pool'. Good luck to all who swim in you."

Elizabella cast a juice carton into the pit. It squelched. "I hoped it would burst ... it's how they do it with boats." She stood back, taking in Pit Pool for the first time.

It was murky, yellow, full of debris and it had a sour musk emanating from the surface.

It was _glorious_.

"Sandy, you first," said Elizabella.

Sandy jumped in and started wading, his tongue sticking out with joy like a puppy.

Elizabella stepped into the pool. After a moment's hesitation, Huck stepped in too. Unlike Elizabella and Sandy, he had rolled up his trousers and taken off his shoes and socks first. Ava and Evie kicked off their shoes and joined them.

Soon enough all the kids were getting in and out, splashing around and having the time of their lives.

They threw balls back and forth, and played piggy-in-the-middle. They did handstands. They pretended to be seals and dugongs and sea horses and sea cats, even though sea cats don't exist – they didn't care.

"This is even cooler than the Bilby Creek Fête!" someone yelled.

Even Daphne was in there, although she did make a point of tying her pigtails together up into a bun high on her head so that they wouldn't get wet and said, "No running near the pool!" over and over even though nobody was listening.

Was it the best pool in the world? Goodness, no. Was having *any* pool randomly appear in the school even if it was foul and stinky the best *thing* in the world? Pretty much!

Then the clouds started to come in and the sun began to disappear.

Or at least that's what it seemed like...

A piercing whistle rang through the playground. As the kids scurried out of the pool, Elizabella realized that it wasn't clouds blocking the sun. It was the towering shape of Mr Gobblefrump.

He screamed for what appeared to be a full minute. To the untrained eye walking into this situation it wouldn't have been obvious who had instigated Pit Pool. But this wasn't Mr Gobblefrump's first rodeo. A stunt like this only had one person's name on it – that very name he had just screamed for eternity.

* * *

Elizabella sat in the Think *Very Hard* About What You've Done Corner, reserved for particularly big trouble. It was in Mr Gobblefrump's office, where he kept snow globes with pictures of himself on the shelves behind his chair. Elizabella thought this was a strange hobby. Only ten minutes ago she had been drenched in pool juice, surrounded by her adoring peers. And now she was in a spare uniform from

Lost and Found that was not only way too small, it was also the school *dress*, which Elizabella thought was all types of wrong. Elizabella looked down at the dangly necktie on the dress. The end of the tie was dark and worn like it had been sucked on every day by its previous owner, which it undoubtedly had.

She could hear Mr Gobblefrump in the playground yelling at everyone. He was so angry, his words were jumbling together like a shouty soup. Next he would be in to give her a gold-standard telling off.

Elizabella knew that teachers were never *really* angry. She'd seen it often enough: they'd laugh with one another, then turn to a kid, yell like that kid had just stepped on a kitten, then promptly turn back to the other teacher and start laughing once more. They pretended to be angry during a telling-off in an effort to bring some gravity to the situation. However, Elizabella suspected that Mr Gobblefrump was an exception to the rule and that he genuinely was furious most of the time. Either that or he deserved a Merit Certificate for

Outstanding Performance in the Field of Angriness.

Elizabella thought she'd take advantage of this quiet time before the Mr Gobblefrump scream-a-thon to work on another haiku in her mind.

Huck has a nice smile,
A nice personality
And he has nice ears

She blushed. *Why am I embarrassed? I am embarrassed for admitting I like Huck in front of my own brain! OMG... Did I just tell myself that I like Huck? Like* like *like?*

And with that, Elizabella scrunched up the thought like a piece of paper and tossed it into her mind-bin, put the mind-bin into a mind-cannon and shot it into mind-space where it could never make her blush again.

Chapter Three

When Elizabella got home that afternoon her dad was in the garden, covered in dirt with a big grin on his face. "Look, Elizabella!" He beckoned her outside. "Mum's waratah!"

Elizabella knew that her mum, Audrey, had grown up in a tiny apartment. When she moved in with Elizabella's dad, it was the first time Audrey had ever lived somewhere with a garden. She loved the garden, but she was hopeless when it came to growing anything in it. Audrey had tried planting basil and parsley, daisies and poppies. But she was easily distracted from the task of nurturing the plants, and whatever she planted inevitably ended up shrivelled and brown – if it ever emerged from being a seed in the ground at all.

Once, for her birthday, Martin had planted Audrey a waratah shrub. He'd said it was hers to look after because it was the type of plant that would thrive even if you might accidentally neglect it from time to time. Elizabella's mum had loved that waratah and it *did* thrive, even though she forgot about it often. It thrived now, even though she had passed away. Elizabella's mum was up in the sky somewhere along with Gran, all the worms that had come and gone from Squiggly Manor and Elizabella's cat Oldcarpetina (named so because when they got her she was already so old she had almost no fur left, and Elizabella thought she resembled a very wise, old carpet).

Elizabella went out into the garden where her dad was proudly pointing to the big red flower coming out of the shrub.

"Mum can still make it flower!" he said.

"Yeah," said Elizabella. "Nice one, Mum."

"Remember when she tried to grow tomatoes and instead she grew an ant colony?"

Elizabella laughed. Her mum had been so bad at growing things. Except for ants. And waratahs. And Elizabellas. She was excellent at growing those. Even her experiment at growing a Toddberry had *something* going for it, Elizabella supposed.

"Now I've worked up a thirst!" her dad said. "Chocolate milkshakes?"

"Sounds great, Dad."

Elizabella followed her dad back inside the house. It was nice to see him so happy and Elizabella's heart sank knowing she was about to really kill the mood by giving him **the letter** that was in her bag... Maybe she'd wait a bit longer.

She sat on a stool by the kitchen bench while her dad got to work on the milkshakes.

"Remember when Mum tore two pairs of jeans and then tried to take the good bits of each pair and staple them together to make a new pair of jeans?" Elizabella asked.

Her dad laughed. "They were the *worst* pair of jeans I'd ever seen!"

"And then she insisted on wearing them to the Bilby Creek Good Time Supermarket just to prove that they worked."

"I was so embarrassed!" said Martin. "I hid in the car while she went in!"

They drank their chocolate milkshakes.

"How was school?" Martin asked.

School was *not* something Elizabella wanted to talk about, because it would quickly lead to the letter in her bag.

She quickly changed the topic. "Let's play snap! I really want to play snap!"

"OK?" said Martin, a tad confused.

Elizabella didn't even like snap. She ran out of the room, cursing herself silently in her head for not suggesting a game she actually *enjoyed*, like gin rummy.

After she returned with the cards, they played a few rounds.

"So, Elizabella, how was school?" her dad asked again.

"Have you done the crossword in the *Bilby Creek Gazette*? We have to do the crossword in the *Bilby Creek Gazette*!" she said hurriedly.

"We do? I didn't know you—"

Elizabella had already run out of the room in search of the paper.

After the crossword, Elizabella suggested sudoku. Then she made her dad read out all the items in the trade and personal sections of the paper, as well as the advice column. He drew the line at the real estate pages.

"Elizabella, I think we've had all the joy we can from the *Bilby Creek Gazette* today," he said.

"Don't you want to see what the median rental price of a two-bedroom apartment in Bilby Creek is?" Elizabella asked.

"Ummm, no," said Martin, closing the paper. "Elizabella, how was school?"

"Well, Dad…"

Her number was up.

A few minutes later, Elizabella was watching her dad's eyes. They would widen, then narrow, as his brows arched and furrowed while he sat at the kitchen table reading the letter that had been sent home with her that day. He was trying to process what Elizabella had done. He was reading the words but he couldn't make them stick together in a comprehensible order. Instead, they floated around his head like balloons randomly bobbing across the sky. *Pool. Gobblefrump. Sandpit. Juice cartons.*

The letter had been transcribed by Mr Biffington, who ran the Bilby Creek Primary School office with his husband, Mr Crab. Mr Biffington and Mr Crab hyphenated their names when they got married on the Gold Coast, so technically they were both Mr Biffington–Crab. To avoid confusion they used their original names at school.

That afternoon, when Mr Gobblefrump had eventually come to see her in the Think *Very Hard* About What You've Done Corner, Elizabella couldn't be too sure exactly what he had said. He had screamed so high, he sounded like an oboe. From outside the office in the playground, Huck, who was waiting for Elizabella, could have sworn he saw a crack appear in the glass of the office window.

After that, Elizabella was taken in to see Mr Biffington, where she had to explain what she had done in full detail. Elizabella loved this; it was like being interviewed for the *Bilby Creek Gazette*. And as Elizabella explained her inspiration, the resources and the sheer human effort involved in the creation of Pit Pool, Mr Biffington had to stifle a Real Human Response.

This was a thing Elizabella had noticed teachers doing all the time. When a kid did something really cool or funny that a teacher didn't want to acknowledge, they would often try to hide their Real Human Response. Sometimes they would fake a coughing fit, make a series of garbled grunts or, in extreme cases, turn around and run away.

Mr Biffington's strategy was to put a handkerchief to his mouth, hiding an involuntary expression of awe, and squint very deeply through his tortoiseshell glasses, masking a look of disbelief. Elizabella was confident that he and Mr Crab would be singing Pit Pool's praises over dinner at home that night.

Now, at the kitchen table, Martin had finally finished the letter. He was starting to grasp what had happened.

"You made a pool ... from juice...?"

"Yeah. I named her Pit Pool."

Martin let out a big sigh.

"Dad, are you OK?" Elizabella asked, as she watched Martin drawing circles around his temples with his fingers.

Then he looked at his watch and sat bolt upright with a start.

"Six thirty!" he cried. "I have to go!" Elizabella was confused. Where could her dad possibly have to go in such a hurry?

"Where?"

"Ahh..." said Martin, already on his feet, "nowhere ... somewhere..."

"What?" asked Elizabella, who had followed him into the bathroom where he was dabbing cologne on his neck. Martin pulled a fifty-dollar note out of his wallet and put it in Elizabella's hands.

"Seeing an action film. Order pizza," he said with a sense of finality. Clearly he had no desire to discuss the matter of his mysterious outing any further.

Why is Dad racing out to see an action film? He never goes to the cinema... But pressing the matter opened the door to more Pit Pool trouble. So, even though it was extremely hard, she swallowed all of her curiosity.

"OK, Dad," she said. "Have fun!" And he promptly left the house. Elizabella went back into the kitchen.

"What about dinner?" said Toddberry, swishing the hair curtains out of his face to reveal a snarl.

He'd been sitting at the kitchen table this whole time, drawing a beast on his forearm. Elizabella looked at Toddberry's inky creation. It was a snake with the head of a dog. Elizabella suspected he had chosen to make the body a snake because it was easier to draw than the body of the dog, but she thought better of suggesting it.

Elizabella pondered the fifty-dollar note scrunched in her fist. *I could order pizza,* she thought, *or I could make Toddberry a special dinner AND give Dad his money back. Win-win!*

"I'll cook dinner," she said.

"What are you going to make? A *picture* of spaghetti bolognaise?" said Toddberry.

Elizabella went to the fridge and started pulling things out. A jar of chocolate spread, two carrots, three leftover spring rolls and anything else that looked vaguely within its use-by date.

She had soon set up a veritable picnic on the table. She put a plate in front of Toddberry and one at her own place. Toddberry stared at dinner which, along with the aforementioned, included strawberry yoghurt, a jar of capers, a cup of cold pea soup and a lettuce leaf. As a final touch, Elizabella put the Sorry Haiku she'd finally settled on in front of him.

Picture was funny
But made Toddberry hungry
For this, I'm sorry

"Thanks," he managed. "It's not, umm ... good, no offence."

"It's a haiku."

"Just because it has a fancy name, doesn't mean it's *good*," said Toddberry.

"It's a Japanese poem with three lines that have five syllables, then seven, then five," she explained.

Toddberry thought for a moment. Then he swished his hair out of his face and started counting on his fingers as he said:

"E-LIZ-A-BEL-LA,

DO YOU CALL THIS MESS DIN-NER?

ME-GA DI-SAS-TER."

Elizabella was impressed. "Wow, you're a really good mean poet," she said.

Toddberry's hair curtains closed, and he mumbled, "I'm good at heaps of stuff but no one knows." He turned his attention back to the feast. "This is literally just the inside of the fridge outside of the fridge."

"Yes!" said Elizabella. "It's Deconstructed Fridge! It's a *delicacy*."

Toddberry and Elizabella ate bits and pieces from Deconstructed Fridge. Well, Elizabella tried to eat a bit of everything in defence of the edibility of her creation, while Toddberry just ate the whole jar of chocolate spread with his finger.

After dinner, she took some of the leftovers outside to Squiggly Manor, the worm farm at the bottom of the garden. She lifted the lid and looked down at the ever-growing worm family. She started scooping in the capers and yoghurt and various other bits and pieces. The curious worms slithered up to the food.

"At least *you* guys have sophisticated palates," she said to the worms. As she watched them begin to gorge on their glorious banquet, she thought about her day. It had been magnificent, of course, but she had ruffled some feathers. Toddberry was surly, even though she had written him a Sorry Haiku and also made him dinner. And on the way home from school, Huck, who had waited for her, said that he noticed some of Mr Gobblefrump's hair was falling out, which was quite something given his hair was actually a toupee. She thought he must be really, *really* stressed

SQUIGGLY MANOR

out to be losing his *fake* hair.

Elizabella decided to write Mr Gobblefrump a Sorry Poem. She thought it should sound a little grown-up. So she sat in the garden watching the worms and let her mind go to work.

In the heat of the moment I forget what's what
I forget what's right and I forget what's not
And my actions do become my art
Forgive me for doing what's in my heart

Chapter Four

The next day, Elizabella caught up with Huck while she was walking to school. She was so keen on being on time, she didn't even think for a second about whether or not she liked or *like* liked Huck.

"I can't be late today," she said, almost walking straight past him. Huck, who *never* wanted to be late, let out an audible sigh of relief. Being such good friends with the naughtiest girl in school was exhausting. Elizabella had started power walking;

Huck jogged along to catch up.

"I am not going to do anything that could possibly be interpreted as naughty between now and the Bilby Creek Fête," she said. Then she thought she'd better wind it back. "Or at least for today. Today I am going to be *perfect*."

"Mum says that nobody's perfect," said Huck.

"Well, maybe not literally," said Elizabella, although she did actually plan to be as **perfect as possible.** Elizabella knew this was an ambitious goal, but she also knew that if she aimed that high and fell a bit short, it would still be a big improvement.

When they arrived at school, Elizabella saw Mr Gobblefrump in the playground. She had written the poem on a piece of fancy pink paper that came in a writing set her dad had given her for her birthday. She'd put it in an envelope with a sprig of lavender from her front garden. She was about to run over and give it to him when he caught her gaze. Elizabella saw a lightning bolt of fear flash across his eyes. He promptly turned away.

"He just looked at you like my mum looks at a spider," said Huck.

"Yes, he did," agreed Elizabella. Maybe it wasn't the best time to give him the poem.

"Handball?" asked Huck, pulling a tennis ball out of his pocket and bouncing it on the ground. He bounced the ball quite high on purpose. It landed on a twig and jolted off in another direction. He chased after it, a little embarrassed.

"You go ahead, I'll see you later," called out Elizabella. She'd just had an idea. She went to the tuck shop and stood behind Sandy, who was placing his order for break.

"Two crumpets, please, Miss Duck," he said, handing over a fifty-cent piece. Miss Duck took the coin, smiling as she wrote his order down on a brown paper bag and put it on the pile.

Miss Duck had been running the school tuck shop for twenty years. Her mother ran it before her and her grandmother ran it before that. In fact, Miss Duck's family had been running the tuck shop since records began. Miss Duck had long, brown hair – so

long it touched the back of her knees, but you'd never know because she put it up in a bun on the top of her head. She wore an apron and dress she had made by reconstructing second-hand Bilby Creek Primary School uniforms. Miss Duck was very handy.

Elizabella was next in the queue.

"I thought two crumpets were a dollar now?" she asked Miss Duck.

"They are, but that's all Sandy ever has for break, and he always comes in with just that one fifty-cent piece. I worry if I give him the new price list he might only be able to afford one," she explained. Miss Duck had a heart of melted chocolate.

"Miss Duck, I need a favour," said Elizabella. "Can you give this Sorry Poem to Mr Gobblefrump? Don't tell him what it is or who it's from or he may not open it."

Elizabella handed over the envelope.

"Of course," said Miss Duck. "I'll give it to him when he comes in for his three bottles of orange juice."

"Three?" asked Elizabella.

"He's doing a juice cleanse," said Miss Duck, shrugging.

And with that the bell rang.

"Better fly," said Elizabella to Miss Duck. "I can't do *anything* naughty today."

Elizabella hurried through the playground and ended up fifth in the line for Miss Carrol's class. *Fifth!* she thought. She'd never got in early enough to be that close to the front before. Miss Carrol approached her class line and literally did a double take when she saw Elizabella.

Maybe this really *was* the day Elizabella was going to change?

* * *

Later that morning, Miss Carrol was showing the class different sentences on the whiteboard and asking people to pick out the verbs:

The cow jumped over the moon.

The girl pushed her sister on the swing.

The hamster ran around the wheel.

These are extremely boring sentences, thought Elizabella. If *she* worked for the Department of Education she would make some changes to the syllabus. She could even make these sentences much better just by changing the verbs.

The cow *hurtled* over the moon.

The girl *launched* her sister on the swing.

The hamster *bolted* around the wheel.

And if she changed the objects of the sentences as well, she could make some real zingers.

The cow *hurtled* over the *house.*

The girl *launched* her sister out of a *giant cake.*

The hamster *bolted* around the *universe.*

The hamster bolted around the girl's hair as she

rode her sister's cow out of a giant cake and hurtled around the universe.

"Elizabella?" called Miss Carrol. Elizabella had been daydreaming.

"Jumped! Pushed! Ran!" said Elizabella.

She looked around. Everyone was staring at her.

"We stopped doing verbs five minutes ago," snapped Daphne.

"Oh..." said Elizabella. She looked to the doorway and saw a very, very, *very* tall girl standing there in a pair of pink denim dungarees.

"I was asking you to make some room for Minnie," said Miss Carrol.

In Miss Carrol's class everyone sat in rows at their own little desk. The desk next to Elizabella was empty. Well, it was empty except for Elizabella's pencil case, homework, ringbinder, exercise books, three olives (that had somehow made their way from last night's Deconstructed Fridge into her backpack, then back out of her backpack and onto this desk), four hairy hair elastics and her house keys.

Elizabella believed in the **Waste Not, Want Not** rule. She understood that the rule was to protect the environment and save money; that's why she always fed leftovers to the worms in Squiggly Manor. But Elizabella saw no reason why it shouldn't be extended to include any vacant surfaces in her vicinity. She quickly got to her feet and started rehousing all her things on her own desk.

She was so busy arranging everything that she didn't really listen as Miss Carrol introduced the new girl to the class.

"This is Minnie," said Miss Carrol, who had to look up at her new student to meet her gaze. Minnie was at least twenty centimetres taller than the teacher and her hair was as long as a whole pre-schooler.

"Minnie's family has just moved to Bilby Creek from Beijing, and I know you will all make her feel extremely welcome. Right, Elizabella?"

Elizabella glanced up. She had stuffed the olives

in her mouth (Waste Not, Want Not). She quickly swallowed them and said, "Of course!"

She had forgotten the olives had stones. Elizabella thumped herself on the chest and three olive pips flew out of her mouth and onto Minnie's new desk. Elizabella swiftly wiped them off and gestured welcomingly at the desk.

Minnie had been standing next to Miss Carrol with a shy smile. As she walked out of Miss Carrol's line of sight towards Elizabella, she went cross-eyed and stuck out her tongue, making Elizabella laugh.

"I don't see what is so funny about the word 'thylacine'," said Miss Carrol, who was putting up some facts about the thylacine, or Tasmanian tiger, on the board for their next lesson.

"Sorry, Miss Carrol," said Elizabella. She looked over at Minnie, who was smiling sweetly at Miss Carrol as though she'd never poked her tongue out in her entire life.

"Nice dungarees," whispered Elizabella.

"My new uniform is being specially altered at

the uniform shop because I'm so tall," said Minnie matter-of-factly.

"Wow," said Elizabella. She had *never* heard of anyone having to do that before.

"At least it's just shorts and a T-shirt. It took for ever for them to alter the winter uniform at my last school. It had so many layers because of the snow."

"It *snowed* at your last school?"

"Yeah. Sometimes."

"I've never seen snow," said Elizabella.

"Really?"

"I don't know if anyone at Bilby Creek Primary has."

Minnie looked at her, shocked, as though Elizabella had just told her that no one at Bilby Creek had ever seen a TV.

★ ★ ★

Being a teacher isn't always easy. Everyone knows the feeling of not wanting to go to school, but lots of kids, including Elizabella, don't realize that teachers sometimes have the same feelings. If they could see their teachers in the mornings, they'd probably think of them very differently. Mr Biffington and Mr Crab hitting snooze on their phone alarms over and over again until the last possible moment, Miss Carrol eating chocolate bars for breakfast as a special treat to will herself out of bed...

After all the excitement of yesterday, Mr Gobblefrump had really considered having the day off. This morning he had looked at himself in his bathroom mirror and given himself a pep talk. **"Once more unto the breach,"** he had said to himself, which is what King Henry says to encourage his army to go back into battle in Mr Gobblefrump's favourite Shakespeare play, *Henry V.* It meant "Let's try once more", which is exactly what Mr Gobblefrump was attempting to convince himself to do. He eventually managed to pull himself together. He picked his toupee up off its little stand, gave it a quick brush to disguise the little bits that were falling out, and put it on his head. "You've got this!" he said, looking in the mirror. He fed his cat, Pemberley, mounted his little yellow bicycle and rode to school.

Now, it was ten minutes before break, and Mr Gobblefrump decided to make his way down to the tuck shop before the fray of children hit the playground.

He walked in and saw Miss Duck behind the counter.

"Good morning, Mr Gobblefrump, will that be three bottles of OJ today?"

"Yes, please, Miss Duck," he said. Miss Duck bustled to the fridge and came back with the bottles. He pulled out his wallet and started taking out a ten-dollar note.

"No charge today!" said Miss Duck.

"Oh?"

Mr Gobblefrump had been ordering so much juice that Miss Duck had had to up *her* order at the Bilby Creek Wholesale Super Mega Mart, which supplied the tuck shop. She'd ordered so much orange juice from them that they'd given her a free box of the stuff. Miss Duck thought it was only fair to pass this saving on to Mr Gobblefrump.

She didn't want to embarrass him, so she came up with this reason: "Ah … yes, we have a … ah … 'buy twelve orange juices get three free' special this week and you've bought enough to redeem!"

"Right … thanks?" said Mr Gobblefrump.

"I also have something else for you," said Miss Duck, and she reached into the pocket of her blouse behind her apron and pulled out Elizabella's letter.

"What's this?" Mr Gobblefrump asked, as she handed it to him.

"Oh, it's something special," she said. "Open it in private." Miss Duck gave him a little smile.

"OK…" said Mr Gobblefrump, a little baffled. He stuffed the letter into his breast pocket, next to the precious Bilby Creek Primary School Rule Book, and picked up the three bottles.

Back in the staffroom he cracked open his first juice and took out the letter. **Mmmm, lavender,** he thought as the scent wafted out of the open envelope.

He read the letter in his head:

In the heat of the moment I forget
what's what
I forget what's right and I forget what's not
And my actions do become my art
Forgive me for doing what's in my heart

"What's that lovely lavender smell?" asked Mr Biffington, who had wandered in.

"Nothing!" Mr Gobblefrump said. He quickly folded the note and put it back in his pocket.

What beautiful verse, Miss Duck! thought Mr Gobblefrump, naturally assuming he was reading her composition.

He had never really thought about Miss Duck in *that* way before. Then again, he never knew she was a poet, and he never, *ever* thought that he, Chester Gobblefrump, would be a poet's muse...

And then there was the matter of the free OJ...

Was it possible Miss Duck was looking to start some sort of courtship?

Chapter Five

During breaktime, Elizabella went to see Miss Duck in the tuck shop.

"One apple, please, Miss Duck, and...?"

"Mission accomplished," Miss Duck said, handing her the apple with a wink.

"Excellent," said Elizabella, giving her fifty cents for the apple. "I owe you one."

Elizabella skipped over to the handball court, where Huck, Ava and Evie were idly bouncing Huck's tennis ball, waiting for Elizabella so they could play a proper game.

"What do you think of the new girl Minnie?" Ava asked the group as she bounced the ball into Huck's square.

"She seems nice. I think she might be a bit shy," said Huck.

"Makes sense," said Evie, "she's moved all the way from *overseas!*"

Evie's right, thought Elizabella. *It must be very hard to move all the way from another country to a place where you don't know anyone.* Even though Minnie hadn't *seemed* very shy to Elizabella when she came over to the desk and stuck out her tongue…

Elizabella looked around for Minnie. She was nowhere to be seen. This was strange. Anyone as tall as her shouldn't be hard to spot in the playground. Elizabella was so distracted that she didn't see Huck whack the ball into her square and, even though it was as slow as honey dripping off a spoon, she completely missed it. The ball bounced up and hit her in the chest.

"Yes!" said Huck, advancing to her square and sending Elizabella down to the bottom position.

Elizabella snapped out of it. As soon as the ball came back to her she slid a low skidding bounce across Ava's square that went so fast Ava barely saw it, let alone hit it with her hand. The twin chased it down the playground.

Sandy came past the handball court and sat in the reserve position on the asphalt.

"No pool today, Elizabella?" he asked.

"No pool today," said Elizabella very seriously.

"How about a bouncy castle made of backpacks? Or we could make a pole vault if we tied a bunch of jumpers together and tied them to the two gum trees near the tuck shop?

"No pool, no bouncy castle, no pole vault, nothing," said Elizabella. "Today I am not doing *anything* naughty."

Sandy looked at her, his eyes wide, like she'd told him that his baby brother had just become the prime minister.

As the kids filed back into Miss Carrol's class after break, they heard a scream that was so high it woke up Mr and Mr Biffington–Crab's British bulldog, Ralph, who was asleep under the desk in the school office.

It was Daphne.

"It's gone!" she screamed.

"What's gone?" asked Miss Carrol.

"Fairy-Wren Blue!" Daphne spluttered through her tears. Daphne was holding her Pickles Pencils tin out for all to see – and there it was. Right there between Pea Green and Night Sky was a gap that stuck out like a missing tooth in a pre-schooler's smile. A gap where that perfect Fairy-Wren Blue pencil should have been.

Everyone stared.

This is going to be a BIG deal, thought Elizabella.

"Daphne, it's just a pencil," Sandy said.

"Just a pencil?!" screamed Daphne. *"Just a pencil?!?!"*

"Yeah," he said, "it's just a pencil."

Of course! thought Elizabella. *Sandy has probably never owned a set of Pickles Pencils.*

She was right. He never had. So he didn't know the joy of gazing longingly up and down that rainbow, committing all their delightful names to memory, ranking them in order from most favourite to least most favourite colour.

Still, he has a point, Elizabella thought. *With the way Daphne's going on, you'd think Fairy-Wren Blue was her actual pet bird that had gone missing, not a pencil.*

"Fairy-Wren Blue is *everything*!" Daphne exclaimed. "I literally can't live without it!"

"Now, Daphne, calm down—" said Miss Carrol.

"Calm down? CALM DOWN? Somebody stole my Fairy-Wren Blue!"

"Daphne, let's not make accusations," said Miss Carrol firmly. "You've probably misplaced it."

Daphne looked injured. "Miss Carrol," she said through a waterfall of tears, "I have *never* lost *anything.*"

"OK, everybody sit down," said Miss Carrol, exasperated. "Can everyone go through their pencil cases to see if they have *accidentally* wound up with Daphne's pencil?"

Ava piped up, "I have a Fairy-Wren Blue, but this one is mine."

"How do you know?!" exclaimed Daphne, running over to Ava's desk. She grabbed the pencil out of the twin's hand and examined it. It was about an inch long and covered in so many bite marks you could barely read those precious words "Fairy-Wren Blue" along the side. Daphne dropped the pencil back on the desk like poison ivy.

"It's definitely mine," said Ava. "Sorry, Daphne."

Daphne stormed back to her desk.

Eventually, after everyone had diligently been through their pencil cases, backpacks, trays and everywhere else they could think of, Miss Carrol put an end to the search party.

"We've all had a good look, Daphne," she said. "Now it's time to get on with the lesson."

"But—" Daphne started to protest.

"No 'buts'," Miss Carrol said. "You're most welcome to continue searching for it after school."

Daphne's mouth gaped open and closed like a goldfish. A goldfish who had never seen such injustice.

Miss Carrol went back to her desk and re-gathered herself.

"Now, where were we?"

They were halfway through the lesson on animal extinction that had commenced before break. They had been learning all about the Tasmanian tiger, which had been the biggest known carnivorous marsupial of the modern era. It had been native to both continental Australia and New Guinea, however by the time of colonization, it had become extinct *except* in Tasmania...

"Ah, yes," said Miss Carrol, picking up where she had left off. "What do we call it when a species comes to live *only* in one defined geographical area?"

"Indigenous?" offered Huck.

"Well, yes, that's a good word," said Miss Carrol, "and it's true, all native Australian animals, including the Tasmanian tiger, are *indigenous.*"

"So is the fairy-wren," piped up an unfamiliar voice.

Everyone stifled a giggle except for Daphne, who made an audible gasp. Miss Carrol spun around ready to tell somebody off for deliberately flaring up Daphne.

"Isn't that right, Miss Carrol?" said Minnie, sweet as a lamb.

If it had been anyone *other* than Minnie, Miss Carrol would have called that cheekiness, but given Minnie was new, surely this was just an innocent remark. In fact, Miss Carrol realized, it was a remark that needed rewarding. It was nice to see Minnie beginning to come out of her shell, and impressive that she knew about native Australian birds.

"Correct, Minnie, well done," Miss Carrol said.

Daphne did a double-gasp, not comprehending that this slight was about to go unpunished. Minnie turned to Elizabella and **winked,** then turned straight back to the board and looked at Miss Carrol virtuously. Miss Carrol continued the lesson. Elizabella looked her new classmate up and down, trying to figure her out. She was becoming less and less like anyone Elizabella had ever met before.

"Some species are indigenous to several places. For example, the brown bear is indigenous to North America, however it's *also* indigenous to parts of Europe and Asia. But species like the Tasmanian tiger and the Tasmanian devil, which are only found in one specific geographical location, are *endemic*."

Despite a rocky start, things are actually going quite well, Miss Carrol thought of the lesson she was running. By the time the bell was about to go for lunch everyone had learned the difference between a species being *endemic* and *indigenous*, as well as the difference between being *extinct* and *endangered*. They'd also learned that endangered species are categorised into different groups – starting with *vulnerable*, then *endangered*, *critically endangered*, *extinct in the wild* and finally *extinct*.

Even though animal extinction was very sad, Miss Carrol loved teaching her children about it. She was an animal lover. Before she became a teacher, Miss Carrol had worked for Greenpeace on their *Rainbow Warrior* ship, travelling the seas and helping save the environment. It was very important to Miss Carrol to instil these messages in her students, so that they might grow up to love and protect animals too.

Satisfied that the lesson had gone swimmingly, Miss Carrol looked at her watch. Just twenty seconds before the lunchtime bell. She picked up the whiteboard eraser and started to rub the lesson off the board when ...

SPLAT.

As the eraser made contact with the flat surface, a bright red substance squirted out of it and all over the board. And all over Miss Carrol. She turned to the class, her beautiful white blouse now splattered with red.

The bell rang for lunch. Nobody dared move.

Miss Carrol lifted her shirt sleeve to her nose and took a sniff. *Tomato sauce,* she deduced. *Somebody has filled my whiteboard eraser with tomato sauce.*

Ten minutes later, everyone was still sitting at their desks. Miss Carrol was sitting at hers, too. She had wiped off all the sauce she could with some tissues, and was now waiting for one of her students to fess up. As the sun beat down through the classroom windows, she could feel herself smelling more tomatoey by the second.

"I will say it once more. Nobody is leaving for lunch until someone confesses."

Everyone looked at each other. No one seemed like they were anywhere near close to owning up to this.

Elizabella caught Sandy's eye. *Nice one,* he mouthed at her silently.

She was shocked. *It wasn't me!* she mouthed back.

"So?" asked Miss Carrol, searching around the room until her eyes met Elizabella's, where they lingered. Elizabella was taken aback.

"Miss Carrol, it wasn't me!" she said. "I promise!" But something in Miss Carrol's eyes said that she didn't believe her.

Several other kids were now staring at Elizabella.

"Just admit it," hissed Daphne.

"Miss Carrol?" asked Huck timidly. Her eyes shot to Huck, expecting him to own up to the crime, or at least to being an accomplice.

"Miss Carrol, can I please go to the toilet?" Huck asked.

"No," said Miss Carrol. "Not until somebody has confessed."

"Elizabella, if you did it, just say so. You don't want Huck to wee himself!" said Sandy.

Elizabella suddenly started to doubt herself. *Did I do this?* She couldn't for the life of her think of anyone else who might have pulled something like this off. But surely if she *had* done something like this in the last four hours she would have remembered? Also, she had *promised* herself that she wasn't going to do anything naughty today.

Elizabella saw Huck's leg shaking, the international sign of somebody about to wee their pants. And she had a terrible thought...

Was it possible that some time ago – weeks, even months – she had loaded the offending eraser with tomato sauce, and Miss Carrol hadn't happened to use that particular eraser until now? There was a surplus of erasers in the classroom, and Elizabella supposed that on a *particularly* naughty day she could have done something like this, then become distracted by something more pressing, completely forgotten about it, and then, well, the rest was history.

She glanced over at Huck. A little bead of sweat had started to roll down his face. She couldn't stand it any more.

"I did it!" she blurted out. Everyone stared at her. Half of them relieved, the other half annoyed.

"All right, everyone, go to lunch," said Miss Carrol coolly. They all started for the door, led by Huck, who danced from one foot to the other in the international dance of not allowing any wee to come out.

Elizabella remained in her seat, aware that she was not who Miss Carrol was addressing just now when she'd sent everyone off to eat. Miss Carrol looked at her.

"Gobblefrump," she said. Elizabella nodded solemnly. She packed up her things and walked herself out the door. She went down to Mr Gobblefrump's office. As she approached his door she let out a loud sigh. He may not have even read the Sorry Poem, and at any rate, it would be meaningless now.

With a heavy heart she knocked on his door.

"Come in!" bellowed Mr Gobblefrump.

Chapter Six

Elizabella had a sick feeling in her stomach. She knew exactly what was coming and she was dreading it. She wasn't even sure whether she'd done anything wrong, but it didn't make her *feel* any less guilty.

Mr Gobblefrump was sitting at his desk at the front of his office. Elizabella noticed the three empty juice bottles. Mr Gobblefrump had ripped the label off one of them, rolled it into a long, sticky strip, and then smooshed it into what Elizabella could have sworn was ... a love-heart shape?

He looked up at her. Elizabella braced herself.

"Come, come sit down," he said, without the slightest hint of anger. Elizabella was very confused. Was it possible he had amnesia and had completely forgotten yesterday's events?

"Mr Gobblefrump, Miss Carrol sent me here..." she started.

"Yes, yes, go on," said Mr Gobblefrump. He was evidently distracted by something in his notepad, which he had been scribbling in.

Elizabella thought she'd better get it over with. "Well, you see, I don't remember doing this, I really don't, but all available evidence suggests that at some point I squeezed some tomato sauce into one of Miss Carrol's whiteboard erasers and then when she went to use it to wipe a lesson off the board, tomato sauce went everywhere. All over the board, all over Miss Carrol's white blouse. Everywhere."

Mr Gobblefrump wasn't paying any attention to her. He was staring away into the middle distance.

She tried to gauge his response. Usually Mr Gobblefrump was very easy to read, but today he was inscrutable.

He pushed his chair away from the desk, stood up and went to the window. He glanced out into the playground, at the children playing handball, eating muesli bars and skipping rope as the sun shone down on Bilby Creek.

"Marvellous day," he said.

"Sorry?"

"I said it's a simply marvellous day. Wouldn't you agree?"

Elizabella looked around; she wasn't sure what was going on. She glanced down at the desk where Mr Gobblefrump had left his notepad. It was covered in doodles of love hearts, flowers and rainbows.

"I said, wouldn't you agree, Elizabella?"

"Yes!" said Elizabella quickly.

"It seems a bit sad to spend such a lovely day cooped up in here, doesn't it?" Mr Gobblefrump continued.

"Yes…" she said again, hesitantly.

Was this a trap?

"How about you run outside and bask in the sunshine with everybody else?"

Now Elizabella was downright concerned. "Are you feeling OK, Mr Gobblefrump?"

"Never better, Elizabella," he said. "Never better."

Getting up very slowly, Elizabella backed out of the doorway. She closed it behind her and stood there, trying to work out what had just happened.

★ ★ ★

From the handball court, Ava, Evie and Huck saw Elizabella coming towards them.

"Oh no," said Huck. "I hope she's OK."

"It's hard to imagine Mr Gobblefrump getting angrier than he was yesterday, but if anything was going to do it ..." said Ava.

"... this would have been it," said Evie, finishing her sister's sentence.

Elizabella reached her friends. They noticed she looked different, somehow.

"Elizabella! Are you all right?" asked Huck.

"Yes, I think so," said Elizabella. "That was the strangest thing ever."

"Did he roll on the floor screaming like a baby?" asked Ava.

"Did he run around in circles screaming, beating his chest with his fists?" asked Evie.

"Did Mr Gobblefrump scream himself to sleep?" asked Huck.

"No," said Elizabella. "He didn't scream *at all*."

The questions came thick and fast from everyone.

"Did he shout?"

"Shriek?"

"Did he howl at his desk lamp like a wolf at the moon?"

"I bet he wailed."

"I bet he yelped liked Mr Biffington and Mr Crab's British bulldog, Ralph!"

"No," said Elizabella slowly. "He didn't scream or shout or shriek or *anything*." She continued, "He was so distracted by something that he barely heard what I said. He was *happy*."

"Mr Gobblefrump? Happy?!" Ava was shocked.

"Yes, he just kept talking about what a nice day it was outside and then he told me to go out and play."

"Do you have any idea why?" asked Evie.

"None. I *did* give him a Sorry Poem for yesterday, but I don't even know if he's read it. And even if he has, it wasn't *that* good."

Everyone fell silent. Even though they all wanted to ask Elizabella the same question, none of them could quite bring themselves to spit the words out.

"I know what you're wondering," said Elizabella.

"Well…" said Evie.

"Did you?" said Ava.

"Honestly," said Elizabella, "I don't think that I did."

They looked at her, unsure what to say.

"When we were sitting there, I was really thinking about it. *Could* I have possibly planted that eraser weeks ago and completely forgotten about it? But I searched my brain far and wide, and I really have no memory of it," said Elizabella.

They all sat there silently for a moment.

"I believe you," said Huck, smiling.

"Same!" said Ava and Evie in unison.

"Thanks, guys," said Elizabella, relieved.

Sandy came over to the handball court. "Nice prank today, Elizabella!" he said.

"She didn't do it!" said Huck, Ava and Evie together.

"Sheesh, OK!" said Sandy. "Whoever did do it is *some* prankster," he said. Then he picked the tennis ball off the ground. "We playing or what?"

★ ★ ★

Mr Gobblefrump had spent several more minutes in his office staring at the dappled sunlight coming through the two big eucalyptus trees by the tuck shop. He was psyching himself up to speak to The Poet. He had been turning what he thought were Miss Duck's words over and over in his mind:

In the heat of the moment I forget
what's what
I forget what's right and I forget what's not
And my actions do become my art
Forgive me for doing what's in my heart

Now all he wanted to do was march down to that school tuck shop and ask Miss Duck if he could take her out to dinner. *Should I…? Shouldn't I…?* His mind kept turning over the same question again and again. And then another phrase came into his head: **carpe diem.** Which meant, "Seize the day!" That's precisely what Mr Gobblefrump decided to do. He rearranged his toupee for luck and marched out of his room, into the playground and straight to the tuck shop.

He was about to declare his intentions there and then on the spot when he remembered it was lunchtime and as such the tuck shop was swarming with children. He got into line and waited. And waited. Slowly advancing in the queue for what felt like an age. Eventually he reached the front and a somewhat frazzled Miss Duck, who was coming to the end of a busy lunchtime shift.

"Can I help you, Mr Gobblefrump?" she asked.

"You may be the only person who can," he said.

Miss Duck did not catch his drift.

"Oh?" she said, one eye already moving to the kid behind him, ready to take her order. Whatever Mr Gobblefrump wanted, if he was going to dally she was going to keep serving, or else she may not get out of there until dinnertime.

"One cherry ice cream, please," the kid behind Mr Gobblefrump placed her order. Miss Duck went to fetch it.

Mr Gobblefrump stood there. Asking Miss Duck out on a date in front of all these children was going to be difficult.

"You see, I feel an urge to eat something," he continued.

"Next!" she called, ignoring him while he made up his mind. Mr Gobblefrump stood to one side at the front of the queue so Miss Duck could keep serving.

"One packet of peanuts, please," another kid ordered.

As Miss Duck was rummaging around for the last of the peanuts, Mr Gobblefrump continued.

"With you," he said.

Miss Duck froze. Could she have heard what she thought she heard? She handed the kid the peanuts, and they gave her eighty cents. There was just one person left in the queue.

"A packet of sultanas like usual, Samuel?" asked Miss Duck.

"Yes, please, Miss Duck," said the little boy from Reception. They exchanged money for sultanas. As Samuel skipped out, Miss Duck noted that Mr Gobblefrump didn't even tell him off for skipping.

The end-of-lunchtime bell rang.

"Did I hear you correctly, Mr Gobblefrump…?" Miss Duck asked hesitantly.

Mr Gobblefrump began to speak slowly. "Ould-way ou-yay ike-lay o-tay o-gay o-tay inner-day ith-way e-may onight-tay?"

"Mr Gobblefrump," said Miss Duck quietly, "there are no more children here. You don't need to speak in pig Latin."

"I know," said Mr Gobblefrump. "It's just something that happens when I get nervous."

"You speak in pig Latin?"

"Es-yay..." he said, looking down, embarrassed.

"Mr Gobblefrump?" said Miss Duck. "Es-yay."

Mr Gobblefrump's eyes lit up and his moustache started twitching.

"Es-yay you will go to dinner with me tonight?" he clarified.

"Es-yay," said Miss Duck again.

"Well!" said Mr Gobblefrump, who hadn't really thought much past this move. "OK then!"

And with that he marched straight back out of the tuck shop.

"Mr Gobblefrump?" Miss Duck called out to him.

Mr Gobblefrump poked his head back inside. "Yes?"

"Ummm... What's the plan?"

"Huh?"

"For tonight?"

He had no plan at all.

"I'll pick you up at eight," he said, because that's

what every man in every film he had ever seen said when he asked out a lady.

"OK, I'll see you at eight," said Miss Duck.

He started to leave again.

"Mr Gobblefrump…?" she called to him gently.

"Yes, Miss Duck?"

"My address," she said, and quickly wrote down her address in the notepad where she took tuck shop orders. She ripped it out and handed it to him. Mr Gobblefrump sure was lucky that Miss Duck had been there to help him ask her out, otherwise he never would have clinched the deal.

When he was outside, Miss Duck heard him say "Goooooo Gobblefrump!" loudly to himself.

What a strange man he is, thought Miss Duck. *Still … a free meal is a free meal.*

★ ★ ★

After lunch, Elizabella's class had a music lesson. This was a relief as she didn't know if she could face Miss Carrol yet, let alone know what she would say to her when she did.

The music teacher was trying to teach everyone to play "Stairway to Heaven" on the recorder. Elizabella sat at the back and quietly breathed into the instrument, not really playing any notes. Her confusion had given way to curiosity and now her detective hat was on. She really wanted to get to the bottom of what happened, having now completely convinced herself that she *hadn't* been responsible for the tomato sauce eraser. Who could it have been? Obviously none of her friends. Certainly not Daphne... Someone in Miss Carrol's class the year before? How long could tomato sauce stay in liquid form inside a whiteboard eraser before it dried up? When would it start to smell? Surely at some point it would start to attract ants...

By the time the bell rang signalling the end of the day, Elizabella was no closer to an answer. And she was certainly no closer to knowing how to play

"Stairway to Heaven" on the recorder.

When she got out to the playground, Minnie was standing there, waiting for her.

"Elizabella," she called to her.

"Oh, hi, Minnie."

"Listen," Minnie continued. "I know you didn't put tomato sauce in the eraser."

Elizabella paused.

"I know you didn't do it … because I did it."

Elizabella's eyes widened. "*You* did it?" She was genuinely shocked.

"Yep. Thanks for taking the rap. I owe you one."

Elizabella didn't know what to say.

"You have proven yourself to be a good Prank Soldier," Minnie said.

Elizabella found herself feeling a little offended. She wasn't anyone's Prank *Soldier*, just yesterday she had created an entire pool!

"I'm not a soldier," said Elizabella. "I'm a Prank *Master* … or *Constable* … wait, what's higher than Soldier?" Army officer titles were not Elizabella's speciality.

"The highest active rank in your nation's army is General," said Minnie.

"Well, I'm that," said Elizabella.

Minnie shrugged. "Gotta go," she said, "I'm off to put drawing pins in the hula hoops so they prick people when they take them for a spin."

Elizabella gasped in horror.

"Just joking!" said Minnie with a laugh. "I'm not *evil*."

Relieved, Elizabella smiled.

"See you tomorrow," said Minnie.

As Minnie turned around to leave, Elizabella noticed she had wrapped her long black hair into a bun. And stuck through the bun was none other than a Fairy-Wren Blue Pickles Pencil!

Chapter Seven

When Elizabella got home from school she went straight to the fridge. She needed to eat something to process everything that had happened. What was good processing food? She settled on fairy bread. She went to the breadbin and pulled out two pieces of fluffy white bread, then pulled the butter out of the fridge and the hundreds and thousands out of the pantry. Then she had another thought. *What if I use strawberry jam instead of butter? That would*

make the tastiest fairy bread in the entire world! She sat down at the dining table with her Extreme Fairy Bread, making a mental note to copyright that name, and started to think.

Her dad, Martin, came in from the garden where he'd been watering hydrangeas and feeding worms. Larry the Lizard was perched on his shoulder. When she saw her dad she half expected to get in trouble, which is why she was surprised when he simply said, "Elizabella! How was your day?"

Of course Martin didn't know anything of what had gone on, and really, Elizabella hadn't got in all that much trouble. Martin noticed the Extreme Fairy Bread (although of course he didn't know that's what it was called; nobody would until Elizabella released her first cookbook, which would be at least ten years from now). He knew that Elizabella sometimes ate fairy bread when she had thoughts to sort through, so he sat down with her at the table.

"What's on your mind, my darling?" he asked.

"Dad, what would happen if somebody did something naughty, and you took the blame for it?"

Martin remembered something that had happened back when he was a student at Bilby Creek High School.

"You know, that's exactly what your mum did for me!"

"Really?" asked Elizabella. She loved hearing stories about her mum.

"Yes!" said Martin, excited by this memory. "Back in English class in Year Twelve, I had snuck a caramel milkshake into the room after lunch. I was slurping at it behind my copy of *Romeo and Juliet*, which we were reading at the time. Now, as you know, Elizabella, *Romeo and Juliet* is often considered to be the greatest love story ever told."

Elizabella nodded. Even though she hadn't read *Romeo and Juliet*, she got the gist. Two teenagers fall in love, their love is forbidden because their families hate each other, blah blah, everybody dies. She was pretty sure most Shakespeare plays ended with blah blah, everybody dies.

Her dad continued: "The teacher asked Bobby Grim what he thought the meaning behind Romeo and Juliet's relationship was, and he said – get this – that they were *faking* being in love to get presents! Imagine that! It doesn't even make any sense! No one was going to get them any presents – everyone was trying to split them up! Anyway, I was so shocked by this ridiculous idea that I involuntarily spat out a giant mouthful of caramel milkshake, right on the back of Bobby Grim's head, which was right in front of me."

Elizabella was enthralled. "Then what?" she asked.

Martin smiled. "The teacher, who had been scrawling on the blackboard, turned around and saw what had happened. I was just about to confess when your mother, who was sitting next to me, piped up. 'That was me, I'm sorry!' she said, sweetly as a kitten. 'You?' The teacher couldn't believe it – because of course your mother never did anything wrong, or at least she never got caught. **Your mum looked at me and winked.** I didn't know what to say. The teacher sent her out to see the principal and as she walked outside I think I fell in love right there."

Elizabella took this all in. She wasn't exactly looking to fall in love with Minnie, but she *would* like to be like her mum…

Suddenly Martin looked a bit concerned. "Elizabella, you haven't let someone take the blame for something you did, have you?"

"No!" said Elizabella. "Still, say that I *had*, isn't that what *you* did? And therefore legally you couldn't get me in trouble for doing the same thing?"

"Elizabella, that's not how the law works. And also, haven't you heard of 'do as I say, not as I do'? It's every parent's right to tell you what's right and wrong even if they haven't always followed the rules themselves."

"That's a silly rule," said Elizabella. "Besides, it's not what happened. It was actually the other way round."

"Ha-ha," a sarcastic laugh could be heard through Toddberry's hair curtains. He'd been sitting privately playing noughts and crosses with himself on his arm.

"It's true!" said Elizabella.

Why wouldn't anyone believe that *someone else* was being naughty for a change?

★ ★ ★

Mr Gobblefrump couldn't read the time on his digital clock as it had fogged up with steam from his cooking. He wafted the steam away with his oven-mitted hands, then realized his glasses had fogged up too. So he took them off and wiped them down, only to find the clock had fogged up once more. Eventually he thought to open the kitchen window, which slowly cleared the steam from the clock. He realized it was seven o'clock. *Seven o'clock!* Mr Gobblefrump only had one hour to prepare everything, tidy the house *and* collect Miss Duck! This was going to be tight.

As he left his stroganoff to simmer and began chopping up the apples and celery for the Waldorf salad, he realized that he hadn't even asked Miss Duck if she had any dietary requirements. Or allergies! Or aversions! Did she have any false teeth?

He sliced through a hard piece of apple and glanced over at the walnuts... He suddenly had an image of her trying to bite through all the crunchy elements of the salad, and a set of false teeth flying across the dining room. This could be a disaster!

There was no time to worry about that now. He went to his bedroom and put on the outfit he had been planning: a pair of neat denim jeans and a purple button-up shirt. He considered himself in the mirror, pleased. *I look like a beetroot,* he thought. *And I LOVE beetroot!*

★ ★ ★

Elizabella had been following her dad around the house all night demanding more **Mum Stories.** Elizabella knew lots of things about her mum – she was messy, she was a terrible gardener, she would stick up for you and she liked reading. But Elizabella always wanted to hear more about her. And the more she learned, the more she *wanted* to learn. She had a picture of her mum in her head and with each story the picture grew bigger and brighter.

Tonight she'd learned more about the little apartment where her mum had lived before she moved in with Elizabella's dad. It was so small it didn't even have an oven, just an electric frying pan, which she used to make omelettes. Omelettes were Audrey's favourite thing because you could eat them for breakfast, lunch and dinner. She made savoury omelettes and sweet ones, too.

"Name me something that doesn't go with egg!" Audrey would say to Martin. He could think of a hundred things, but would always say, "Nothing, my darling," and lovingly eat whatever she had concocted, even if it made him gag.

"Yep, she loved a kitchen experiment, your mum, just like you!" said Martin now. Elizabella beamed.

"Don't remind me," groaned Toddberry, swishing his hair out of his face briefly, revealing a sour expression. "When I asked for a gingerbread house for my sixth birthday cake, she made me a regular bread house instead," he said, shuddering at the memory.

"Yes, look, it *was* a bit structurally unsound..." Martin said.

"When she put the candles in the whole thing collapsed *and* caught fire!" said Toddberry.

"Cool!" said Elizabella, mentally adding a

smashed-up house made out of soft white bread set ablaze to the ever-expanding picture of her mum. She couldn't wait to make one herself.

* * *

Miss Duck had showered and powdered and plucked and perfumed and was ready for Mr Gobblefrump to come and pick her up. Now she sat in the front room, peeking through the curtain and impatiently waiting for her date.

Even though Miss Duck had been fairly indifferent to dinner with that strange fellow, Mr Gobblefrump, a few hours before, as she got herself ready, she felt herself becoming all aflutter. She glanced at her watch. 7.55 p.m. *One more trip to the toilet?* she asked herself. *Yes, one more should see him arrive.* And just as she'd got all the clothing down required to do her business, she heard the doorbell ring.

DING DONG

"Fiddlesticks!" she hissed to herself as she finished and tried to pull her tights up with both speed and also the carefulness required to ensure she didn't snag them and create ladders.

She answered the door. There stood Mr Gobblefrump in a big purple shirt with a little sprig of lavender affixed to the breast pocket.

Mr Gobblefrump looked at her, wearing bright red lipstick and a lovely dress that was covered in pictures of cats wearing sunglasses. He had never seen her out of her school uniform apron before.

"Miss Duck, you do look ravishing," he said.

Miss Duck blushed. "Thank you, Mr Gobblefrump," she replied. "Now, where are we off to? The Sailor's Inn? Ristorante Ferrari?"

"No, tonight we will dine at a brand-new restaurant!" he declared.

"Oh?" she said, curious.

"Yes, its opening has been widely anticipated in the food section of the *Bilby Creek Gazette*."

"Really?" said Miss Duck, who was getting very excited. What could this place be?

Mr Gobblefrump paused for a moment.

"It's called Chez Gobblefrump!"

"Oh…" said Miss Duck, a little disappointed. She saw a flash of pain on his face. "I mean… Oh, goodie! I hear great things about that establishment!"

Mr Gobblefrump beamed.

"And where is your car?" she enquired innocently.

"You shall be transported via the most romantic vehicle of all."

Miss Duck looked around for a horse and carriage, or at the very least a Cadillac. Then she saw it.

"Oh no…" she said, this time unable to mask her feelings.

"It's a bicycle built for two!" said Mr Gobblefrump, proudly gesturing to his wheels. He'd bought the thing many years ago at a vintage fair, but had never had cause to use it before. And he hadn't really thought about whether Miss Duck had any degree of bicycle proficiency.

He was about to find out!

Chapter Eight

Miss Duck somehow mounted the bicycle with a lot of assistance, but was unable to keep it steady while Mr Gobblefrump climbed aboard. Eventually, Mr Gobblefrump propped the thing against a tree so that once Miss Duck was on it, it could not move. Now, finally, they were on their way – despite having seven near-crashes before either of the wheels were in motion, which must have been some sort of record.

Mr Gobblefrump was astonished to learn that

Miss Duck had *never* ridden a bike in her entire life. As he peddled down the street, he was all too aware of what felt like ten bee stings piercing his back. It was actually Miss Duck's fingernails.

Away they rode, Miss Duck with her **eyes pinched shut** and her **knuckles white,** Mr Gobblefrump trying not to yelp every time the woman changed her grip. For one brief moment, Miss Duck had opened her eyes and allowed herself to feel the wind in her hair as they rode through Bilby Creek Square. She almost, *almost* enjoyed herself for a second. Then the fear flooded back in and she gripped onto Mr Gobblefrump's back even tighter.

The dismount was less graceful than the mount, but at this point all decorum had gone out the window. Miss Duck wanted off, whatever it took, as quickly as possible. She walked slowly and bow-leggedly up to Mr Gobblefrump's front door. He was several steps behind her.

Half an hour later, they were sitting at the dining room table. Miss Duck was recovering. She had got to the bottom of a glass of water and could feel her heart resume a more human pace.

Now she was ready for her date.

"How about something a bit stronger?" she called to the man in the kitchen.

He was delighted. "Coming right up!"

Mr Gobblefrump pulled a bottle out of the fridge, dramatically popped the cork, which flew across the room and hit a picture of his dear old mother right in the eye, and poured two glasses of sparkling red wine. Then he went to the sound system and put on the Romantic Hits To Make Her Swoon compilation he'd purchased at the Bilby Creek Good Time Supermarket that afternoon, before coming back to the table.

"Cheers!" he said, raising his glass to Miss Duck.

"Cheers," she replied, taking everything in. Miss Duck couldn't help feeling a little bit girly about the effort that somebody was going to just for her.

Mr Gobblefrump had everything ready: the salad was prepared, the stroganoff was simmering, the ice cream – well, that was waiting in the freezer to be scooped out when the time came for it to play its part. This was going extremely well. All that was needed was some witty conversation and they'd really be in business. Of course, as soon as he'd had that thought, **his brain turned to mashed potato.**

"So, ahhh, Miss Duck…"

"Please, call me Petunia," she said.

"Right, Petunia, so, *Petunia*, do you … umm … like … working at the tuck shop?"

"Well, umm, Mr…?" Miss Duck was waiting for an invitation to call Mr Gobblefrump by his given name, but he was so nervous it took him a moment to pick up on the hint.

"Chester!" he exclaimed eventually, as though he had solved a cryptic crossword puzzle. "You can call me Chester."

Miss Duck smiled. "Chester, I do like it very much. The women in my family have been working at the Bilby Creek Primary School tuck shop since television was in black and white."

"Astonishing!" said Chester. "What's your favourite TV show in black and white?"

"There's no contest," said Miss Duck.

"Wait, may I guess?" asked Mr Gobblefrump.

"Was it ... *I Love Lucy*?"

"Yes!" cried Miss Duck.

They both said in unison: "I LOVE *I Love Lucy*!"

And with that, the ice was broken.

★ ★ ★

Elizabella couldn't believe all the awesome things she had learned about her mum in one short night. She wanted to call Huck to tell him about it, but it was after dinner, which meant no phone calls. Of course this was hardly an impediment to Elizabella, who was always able to find solutions to everything, including communication issues. Elizabella walked down to the bottom of her garden and started yelling over the fence.

"Oi, Huck! Huck!!"

"Is that you, Elizabella?" came a woman's voice. It was Huck's mum, Leanne.

"Umm, yes, Leanne. Sorry to yell so late. I just wanted to tell Huck something."

She heard a loud sigh. "OK, make it quick.

Huck has homework to finish."

"Yep, sure thing!" said Elizabella, even though she'd never managed to tell a story quickly in her life, let alone the billion stories she wanted to tell Huck about her mum right now. There was one main thing she wanted to talk about. She'd had an idea...

"Elizabella?" Huck's voice came over the fence.

"Huck, have you thought about what food you're going to make for the Bilby Creek Fête?" Elizabella yelled.

Each year, Miss Duck would have a big spread of food for everyone to eat, and kids were invited to contribute too.

"I thought I might just make some cookies again," said Huck.

"You *could* make cookies..."

"Or...?" yelled Huck, anticipating there was more to come.

"Or you could help me make a bread house?" finished Elizabella.

"You mean a gingerbread house?"

"No, a regular bread house!"

"I don't think that's a real thing," said Huck.

"Oh, it's a real thing. And you set it on fire!"

"Really? It sounds very cool!"

"It is," said Elizabella. "It's a really rare delicacy. I just have to figure out the recipe."

"You don't have a recipe?"

"No, it was my mum's secret, so it was never written down! We'll have to work it out."

"Huuuuuck!" Elizabella heard the distant yells of Huck's mum from inside his house.

"I better go, Elizabella! Good night!" said Huck.

"Good night!" she said, and listened as his footsteps crunching on fallen leaves got quieter and quieter as he neared the back door of his house.

It was a plan.

★ ★ ★

When the stroganoff had gone down a treat, and Miss Duck had made many positive comments about the Waldorf salad despite his earlier concerns, Mr Gobblefrump thought it was high time to bring up the poem.

"Miss Duck, ahh, I mean Petunia, I, ahh, um, must talk to you about your words."

"Excuse me?" said Miss Duck, thinking perhaps Mr Gobblefrump had thought she had said something rude.

"Your words, Petunia! Your marvellous verse!"

Now she was truly lost. What *was* he talking about?

"In the heat of the moment I forget what's what," said Mr Gobblefrump in his best voice, staring into Miss Duck's baffled eyes. *"I forget what's right and I forget what's not…"*

Well, now, it seemed the gentleman had truly **taken leave of his senses.**

"Petunia, when you handed me that envelope, I had no clue what was inside. Then when I opened it and breathed in that lavender," Mr Gobblefrump touched the lavender in his pocket, "this very lavender that I have attached to my breast, and then

I read the beautiful words you had composed..."

Oh no... The penny had finally dropped for Miss Duck. *He thinks that poem was from me! And a love poem at that!*

Mr Gobblefrump continued to recite, keeping his eyes locked with hers, *"My actions do become my art, forgive me for doing what's in my heart."*

And with that he began to lean his body over the table with an unexpected daintiness. *He's offering himself up for a kiss!* thought Miss Duck. *He's offering himself up for a kiss, and … and I like it!* And she leaned across to meet him in the middle and planted a delicate kiss on Mr Gobblefrump's cheek.

★ ★ ★

Elizabella was lying on her bed thinking about her mum, remembering the things she used to do like eat ice cream with her fingers and do all the voices when she'd read Elizabella a story. If it was a fairy story, her mum would often point out the bad bits and together she and Elizabella would find a way to fix them. She remembered one time when they were discussing how to fix *Rapunzel*. Her mum pointed out that the prince could have at least bought Rapunzel a fancy hair treatment, to deal with the inevitable split ends that would have come from climbing all the way up her hair. She and her mum had been improvising a scene between the prince and Rapunzel when her mum had got excited and grabbed the book with her ice-cream-covered fingers, coating it in chocolate goo. Elizabella had gasped.

"Don't worry, darling," her mum had said. "I have a magic stick!" Her mum had gone to the laundry room and come back with a big, sticky, orange stick. She rubbed it all over the book, and all over Elizabella's nightdress, which had also caught some of the ice cream deluge. And in an instant the mess was gone.

"Wow!" said Elizabella.

"This is my magic stain stick," her mum explained. "It gets out *everything*. Ice cream, mustard, tomato sauce..."

Tomato sauce! Elizabella shook herself out of her memory and went to the laundry and started rummaging around the cupboards. There was a lot of stuff in there. Toddberry's old socks, a broken dustbuster, dead lightbulbs, used lint rollers … and then she saw it. Her mum's orange magic stain stick. She grabbed it and ran out of the room.

She stomped down the hall, so loud and fast that Toddberry heard it through his deafening headphones and came out of his room to see what the commotion was about.

"What's up with you?" he asked as his sister flew by.

Elizabella barely heard him. She went to her room, pulled out her *best* silver writing paper and a ruby red pen, and began to write.

★ ★ ★

Sitting on her couch, watching some reality TV and idly making some seashell necklaces to sell at the Bilby Creek Fête, Miss Carrol heard a rustling out the front. *Curious,* she thought. She went outside to investigate and glimpsed a hand close her letter box then scurry away into the night. She went over to it and discovered a little lumpy envelope...

Dear Miss Carrol,

I know you probably won't believe me, but I truly didn't put the tomato sauce in your eraser. I thought for a moment that maybe I had done it and forgotten, but after a lot of thinking I realized I really didn't. And I now know who did it, but I can't say who. And please don't ask me because I won't dob them in. And if that makes me just as bad, well so be it.

I was going to write you a Sorry Poem. Instead I found this magic stain stick. My mum used to use it to get anything out. It really works, trust me, she was the messiest woman on the planet.

Anyway, I'm sorry about your lovely shirt.
xxx Elizabella

Miss Carrol peered into the envelope and pulled out a stubby little orange stick wrapped in a ribbon.

Chapter Nine

Elizabella and Huck had just arrived at school. This was Take Two of her attempt to be perfect for a day, as she'd explained to Huck as they walked there.

"Elizabella!"

They both looked over to see Miss Duck frantically gesturing for Elizabella to come over to the tuck shop.

"I better go see what that's about," she said to Huck.

When Elizabella got to the tuck shop, Miss Duck started trying to explain what had happened the night before. There was so much to communicate and she started getting tongue-tied, struggling to separate the important bits of the story from the little details.

"And there was a bicycle built for two … and then the salad with all the nuts and … and … he thinks the Sorry Poem *you* wrote for *him* …"

Elizabella was starting to understand. "… was actually a love poem *you* wrote for *him*!"

"Yes! And I didn't know what to say so I didn't say anything! And then … and then…"

"What, what?" Elizabella asked.

"And then I kissed him on the cheek!" Miss Duck cried.

"Ewwwwwwwww!" said Elizabella involuntarily. Then, realizing that this may have been insensitive, she said, "I mean … good? Was it nice? Are you happy?"

"Oh, Elizabella, I don't know. Chester certainly isn't the type I would normally go for," said Miss Duck.

"Chester?!" spluttered Elizabella, trying to come to terms with the fact that Mr Gobblefrump had a first name.

"Now I feel such a fraud."

Elizabella looked into Miss Duck's eyes. Who was she to deny the lady some happiness, even if it was with … **Chester.**

"Miss Duck, some very famous people have ghostwriters. It means having a silent partner who does the writing for you. It's a legitimate thing. Let me write you another poem."

"Oh no, I couldn't possibly…" said Miss Duck.

"It's already composing itself in my head," Elizabella lied. How in the name of Banjo Paterson was she going to write a love poem to Mr Gobblefrump?

The morning bell rang and Elizabella went straight to her class line. When she clamped eyes on her teacher she realized Miss Carrol was wearing the very same blouse that less than twenty-four hours ago was splattered with a shirt-killing volume of tomato sauce. *The stick must have worked!* thought Elizabella, delighted.

Miss Carrol walked down the line, checking to see if everyone was in place.

"Miss Carrol!" Elizabella cried out. "Your shirt looks perfect!"

"Doesn't it?" said Miss Carrol. "Bit of magic did the trick," she added, smiling. Then she came right up to Elizabella. "Oh and, Elizabella?"

"Yes, Miss Carrol?"

Miss Carrol whispered in her ear: **"I believe you."**

★ ★ ★

That morning Miss Carrol was teaching her class about the different parts of a cell, which is the smallest part or unit in any living organism. They had learned that even though cells could be quite diverse across different animals and plants, they all had certain things in common. No matter if it was a cell in a flea, a flower or a tyrannosaurus rex, all cells have a plasma membrane, cytoplasm, ribosomes and DNA.

Elizabella was drawing the different parts of the cell in her book when she noticed something thin and rainbow-coloured slither onto her desk. It was a giant jelly snake. She looked up and saw Minnie moving her hand away, leaving it there.

"That's to say thanks," Minnie said.

"For yesterday?" asked Elizabella.

"No, for what you're doing with Mr Gobblefrump and Miss Duck. It's genius."

Elizabella was taken aback. Minnie was apparently very good at gathering information.

"I, ahh, don't know what you're talking about," said Elizabella.

"Yes, you do. You're writing love poems for Miss Duck to give to Mr Gobblefrump. I heard you talking to her about it at the tuck shop."

Elizabella had *no idea* anyone had seen her. Minnie was stealthy.

"And why would *you* thank me for *that*?"

"Because if Mr Gobblefrump is happy, nobody gets in trouble," said Minnie. "That's why you didn't get in trouble with him yesterday about the eraser. You're very smart, Elizabella."

Elizabella thought about this. Minnie was right.

If she could keep Mr Gobblefrump happy then maybe she could keep on being Elizabella with *no consequences*. Of course Elizabella was going to write a new poem to help Miss Duck, but was there any harm in being helped herself in the process? An always happy Mr Gobblefrump... That could be a real bonus.

"So, are you going to write another one tonight?" asked Minnie.

"Yes. Yes, I think I will. Don't tell anyone about it, I don't want it to get out and embarrass Miss Duck," said Elizabella.

Minnie put her thumb and index finger together and pulled them across her lips like a zip.

★ ★ ★

"Using stones to weigh down the plastic lining at the bottom was inspired, Sandy," said Elizabella. Sandy didn't seem to be listening.

It was lunchtime and Elizabella was sitting with her friends, reminiscing about Pit Pool.

"I said it was *inspired*," she said again to Sandy, who was completely engrossed in something else.

"Look at the monkey bars!" he said, and pointed to where Minnie sat atop them, her long black hair flying in the wind. She was talking to a small crowd who surrounded her, some on the monkey bars with her, others down below. Even from as far away as they were, it was obvious that everyone was enraptured with whatever she was saying.

"Remember Daphne telling everyone not to run near the pool?" said Elizabella, trying again.

"Shall I go over and see what all the fuss is about?" said Huck.

"No!" Elizabella snapped. Everyone looked at her. It wasn't like Elizabella to lose her cool. She suddenly heard herself in her own head and realized she was starting to sound jealous.

"I mean ... yes, you'd better—"

Before Elizabella could even finish the sentence,

Huck had bolted away to the monkey bars.

"I thought she was so shy, but Minnie doesn't *seem* very shy right now," said Ava.

"Trust me, she's not shy," said Elizabella. "Still, I'm sure it's nothing. What could be that exciting about Minnie sitting on the monkey bars?"

"She's very tall," offered Evie. "Maybe she can stand up and catch cockatoos from there?"

They waited a few minutes for Huck to return with news. He didn't seem to be coming back. The others were getting restless to find out what excitement was in store.

"I think I'll go over to make sure Huck is OK," said Evie.

"Same," said Ava.

"Double same," said Sandy.

And with that, all of Elizabella's little group got to their feet and started to head over.

Sandy turned back to Elizabella. "You coming?" he asked her.

"Nah, I'll stay here, and mind … the hopscotch," said Elizabella.

"Suit yourself!" said Sandy, while dashing over to the monkey bars, which had suddenly become **the new centre of the universe.**

Elizabella sat alone on the HOME segment of the hopscotch court, eating a Vegemite sandwich and feeling a bit sorry for herself. *Wait, what am I doing?* she thought. She had no real reason to be jealous of Minnie. Minnie had done nothing other than try to be friends with Elizabella, really. Minnie was probably just teaching everyone some rude words in Mandarin, which she spoke as well as English. If so, Elizabella should probably learn them too. So she shook off her little cloak of envy and headed over.

At the monkey bars, bits and pieces were being passed up through various hands to Minnie. First a big stick, then a very long piece of string. Elizabella stood by and watched as Minnie attached the string to the stick. *What is she up to?* Elizabella thought to herself. She couldn't work it out.

Kids kept passing up strange little objects: a plastic fork, a pair of compasses... Minnie would examine each of them, holding them to the end of the string and then dismissing them. More things were passed up to Minnie: a pair of sunglasses, some foil shaped like a big U, the lid of a thick black marker pen, a plastic spiral from the spine of an exercise book. Each one was briefly considered by Minnie then rejected. Then someone passed up a small metal slinky. Minnie looked at it and nodded. This was what she wanted. She tied the slinky to the end of the string.

"Irma, Code Gob," she said suddenly. Irma in Year Five nodded at Minnie then skipped across the playground towards Mr Gobblefrump, who (as always) was on duty. Elizabella could see Irma skipping around the man and sort of rounding him up like a sheep.

Without Mr Gobblefrump realizing, Irma was positioning him exactly where Minnie wanted. And when he was in place, Minnie swung the stick out into the air and lowered it so that the slinky was just above Mr Gobblefrump's head. Then, with expert dexterity, she manoeuvred the slinky so that it hooked onto the toupee.

And then she lifted the toupee clean off Mr Gobblefrump's head!

He spun around, patting his bald top, and everyone braced themselves for the incoming storm. Mr Gobblefrump let out a sound...

What was it?

"Aaah... Huh!"

They'd never heard such a sound.

"Huh! Huh! Huh!"

"Is that a ... laugh?" asked Sandy.

"Hee hee hee!" Mr Gobblefrump continued to make these strange new sounds, sounds he barely recognized himself.

"Excuse me?" Elizabella felt something tugging at her shirt. It was Samuel in Reception.

"Mr Gobblefrump is *laughing*?" he asked Elizabella.

"Yes," said Elizabella, stunned. "I actually think he is."

"Good one, kids!" said Mr Gobblefrump with a big smile. "You got me good!"

Elizabella looked up at Minnie, who was staring straight at her.

See? mouthed Minnie. **You're a genius.**

Elizabella smiled up at her.

"Gosh, Minnie has pretty hair," said Huck, who was now standing next to Elizabella and gazing up at Minnie on the monkey bars.

And as swiftly as it arrived, the smile came clean off Elizabella's mouth, like drops of rain swept away by windscreen wipers.

★ ★ ★

Elizabella sat at the dinner table with her dad and Toddberry. Toddberry was there in body alone; his spirit was faraway, deep inside the secret level of *Fierce Frogs IV* he had just unlocked. He sat with his head bent so low in concentration, it was actually resting on the table.

"I think it was kind of mean," Elizabella said to her dad, having explained Minnie's prank that day in some detail.

"But Mr Gobblefrump thought it was funny?" asked Martin.

"Yes!"

"That doesn't *sound* like him," said Martin. "Why do you think he was amused?"

"Because—" Elizabella was about to blurt out about the poem and the misunderstanding and the new romance between Mr Gobblefrump and Miss Duck, then thought otherwise. It was better if this secret remained hers alone. Well, hers and Miss Duck's. And Minnie's...

"Because...?" Martin prompted her to finish.

"Because ... I have no idea, Dad."

"It does *sound* like exactly the type of thing to make Mr Gobblefrump very upset, but if *he* thought it was a good laugh, then I don't see any reason why you should allow it to upset *you*, darling."

"I know, but—"

"You're just feeling *empathy* for Mr Gobblefrump, that's all," said Martin, smiling and giving the giant knot in Elizabella's hair a pull.

Elizabella felt bad. Empathy meant to see something from someone else's perspective and to understand how they were feeling. That's not what Elizabella was doing. Instead, she was **feeling**

jealous. Jealous of the attention Minnie was getting as a prankster and extra, *extra* jealous that Huck had said something nice about Minnie's hair.

Still, Minnie *needed* Elizabella to keep Mr Gobblefrump happy. And so did Miss Duck. There wasn't actually anyone in the school who *wouldn't* benefit from Mr Gobblefrump being pumped full of happiness.

"Thanks, Dad," she said, finishing the last of her ravioli.

Later that night, Elizabella was sitting in her room trying to compose a love poem for Miss Duck to give Mr Gobblefrump. She was tossing ideas around in her head when she suddenly remembered another fairytale her mother had taken issue with. It was *Cinderella*.

Her mum had explained to her: "If a girl wants to leave a party before midnight, that's perfectly fine. And if a prince steals her shoe while she's trying to leave, well, he's a jerk."

Her mum had made a good point. Elizabella jotted it down in a notebook titled *Fixytales*, where she was noting all the fairytales that could be improved with a little editing. Her mum had even helped her write some of them out before she passed away. Together, they wrote under the pen-name Elizamamabella.

"OK ... gross!" Elizabella said to herself as she pulled out a piece of pink paper and drew a giant love heart on it, which would become the border for the poem she was about to write. She started thinking.

Chester, Chester, no one is ... bester?

Hmmm... That sounded more like one of the Bilby Creek Primary School sporting house cheers. And not a good one at that. This was hard.

Then she thought of something:

Real hair is so passé
When you could wear a fine toupee
Who wants frizz or flyaways
Or to get knots or nits or greys?
When atop your head
Where the hairs you've shed
You could wear a very fine toupee.

Yuck, thought Elizabella as she finished the poem. She decided to write something nice for herself to take her mind off things. She decided to pick up on the fixytale that Elizamamabella had never got around to finishing. It was called "The Princess and The Pea or Nobody Likes a Whinger". It began: *Once upon a time, in a world without internet dating, a prince – let's call him Barry – was having difficulty finding true love...*[1]

1. To find out what happens with Prince Barry's search for love, flick to the end of the book now. Or you can read it when you get to the end of *this* story. Or some other time when you're bored. It's your book, I won't tell you what to do!

Chapter Ten

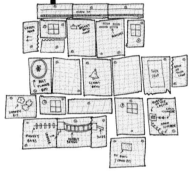

Elizabella walked to school with her love poem in a little envelope all ready to be delivered to Miss Duck. She was busy thinking about what she had written, scuffing her shoes into the dirt and fiddling with her big knot, when someone came up behind her and put their hands over her eyes.

"Guess who?"

"Huck, if you're going to do 'Guess who?' you need to put on a voice, otherwise it's pretty obvious it's

you," said Elizabella.

"OK … a-gueeessss a-whoooooooo?"

"Huck, I don't know what that voice was, but I already know it's you," Elizabella said.

"It was a ghost," said Huck as he moved his hands away. "Elizabella, did you wake up on the wrong side of the bed this morning?"

The truth was that Elizabella's feelings for Huck were getting harder to deny, and the more she liked him, the less she wanted him to know about it.

"No. I'm sorry, Huck," she said.

"That's OK," said Huck. "Wasn't that funny yesterday, when Minnie fished the toupee right off Mr Gobblefrump's head?"

Elizabella stifled a grimace. "Yes, it was," she managed to say.

"I don't know *how* she managed to make Mr Gobblefrump *laugh*, she must be magic!"

At this point Elizabella's eye was twitching. She

130

desperately wanted to tell Huck that it was *her* who had made Mr Gobblefrump happy, not *Minnie*, but she thought that the fewer people who knew about this ruse for the time being, the longer it might last.

When they got to school, Elizabella went to see Miss Duck in the tuck shop. There were a few kids waiting to give their lunch orders.

Elizabella waited for the line to clear so she could deliver the poem.

"Wonderful!" said Miss Duck, after Elizabella had given her a recital. "And you want to know something? I kind of *do* like his toupee."

Elizabella did a big shudder that started at the bottom of her belly and crawled all the way up until her shoulders shook and her face screwed up like she'd just eaten a lemon.

"What's the matter? Are you cold?" asked Miss Duck, concerned.

"No, no, that's ahh ... very nice," said Elizabella. *Miss Duck and Mr Gobblefrump.* The thought of it was gross with a capital everything. G. R. O. S. S.

"I'll give it to him tonight," said Miss Duck. "I'm

going to his house to look at photos of his recent trip to the toothpaste factory."

"That doesn't sound like much fun," said Elizabella.

"I agree," said Miss Duck. "But sometimes you have to humour the people you like."

"Hmmmm," said Elizabella. If being in a relationship meant looking at photos of *anybody's* trip to the toothpaste factory, she might stay single for ever. Elizabella shivered just thinking about it. "Bye, Miss Duck!" she said as she left the tuck shop.

★ ★ ★

In the playground that morning all anyone could talk about was Minnie. Minnie this, Minnie that. And not only were people praising her for yesterday's feats, they were already *making up* stories about her, which meant she was well on her way to legendary status. When the bell rang and Elizabella was lining up for class she heard it going up and down.

"I heard her mum is a spy!"

"I heard she's two metres tall!"

"Minnie has a pet that's a half dog, half parrot, half tree!" said Daphne.

Elizabella couldn't take it any longer. She called out to Daphne, who was first in the line: "Daphne, that's ridiculous. Firstly, how can something have *three* halves?"

Daphne spun around and said, "What's the matter? You *jealous*?"

Suddenly Elizabella could feel **lots of pairs of eyes** on her.

"No!" said Elizabella, way too defensively. "I'm just surprised that you don't know how fractions work, Daphne. I thought maths was supposed to be your *favourite* subject."

There were a few snickers and Daphne looked upset.

Even though Daphne annoyed the living daylights out of her, Elizabella didn't like that she'd been mean to her just now. And she didn't like that she hadn't played along with Huck's "Guess who?" game that morning.

In fact, she didn't like what the presence of Minnie was beginning to do to her at all.

* * *

That morning, after the first bell had gone, Mr Gobblefrump took advantage of the fact that his class was having a lesson in the library to make a visit down to his new favourite place in the whole school – that wondrous building that was the tuck shop. As he traversed the playground, he felt so light, as though his feet were barely touching the ground. Had anybody been there to watch him, they would have sworn he was floating to the tuck shop and not walking at all.

"Petunia!" he sang as he walked in. "Petunia, Petunia, Petunia!"

Miss Duck was a little embarrassed, even though no one else was around to be embarrassed in front of.

"I have another poem for you," said Miss Duck, as she pulled the envelope out of her pocket.

Mr Gobblefrump was thrilled. He took the

envelope and held it under his moustache, which twitched with delight. He took a great big **sniff.**

★ ★ ★

"OK, class, today we're learning about triangles," said Miss Carrol.

"Psst, Elizabella," hissed Minnie. "Is Mr Gobble-head going to be happy again today?"

Elizabella looked over at her. "I wrote another poem, if that's what you mean," she said quietly, so the teacher couldn't hear them.

"Nice work, soldier," said Minnie.

Elizabella flinched. She did *not* want to be Minnie's soldier. And she'd already made that clear.

"Hey, Elizabella," Minnie whispered. "How do you feel about a little teamwork today?"

Elizabella looked at Minnie, surprised. This certainly wasn't what she'd been expecting Minnie to say. Elizabella wanted to tell her to buzz off, but she also wanted to be a Big Person – and, frankly, she was curious. "I'm listening..."

"What are your feelings about handball?"

"Very positive."

And with that, Minnie got to explaining her scheme to Elizabella.

"Elizabella, I need you to describe the playground. Perfectly." Elizabella knew that playground as well as she knew her giant knot, which is to say, extremely well. She carefully described it to Minnie, who had pulled out a protractor, set squares and an exercise book.

While most of the class was busy learning the difference between isosceles, scalene and equilateral triangles, Minnie had been listening intently to Elizabella and drawing parts of the playground perfectly to scale on the pages of her exercise book. Then she tore them all out.

When lunchtime came, Minnie spread the pages out to make one big picture on the concrete behind the tuck shop, where no one could see. Elizabella weighed each page down with rocks. When they finished, they were staring at a big bird's-eye view of the very playground they were sitting in. With one massive difference...

At the four corners of the playground were the four handball courts. But in *this* picture, extra lines had been drawn to join them together to make one giant grid *or* **one giant handball court,** probably the biggest in the world.

Minnie picked up a stick and traced it over the lines on the diagram that connected the handball courts.

"Now what we need is heaps and heaps and heaps of chalk," said Minnie.

"And I know exactly where to get it," Elizabella said. She had spotted Tabitha from Year Six in the playground.

"Tabitha, you're on office duty today, right?" she called out, heading over to her.

"Yeah," said Tabitha.

Every day at Bilby Creek Primary, a different kid from Year Six was the Office Duty Kid. This meant that they spent that day with whichever of the Mr Biffington–Crabs was working, helping out with whatever needed doing in the office – photocopying, taking notes to different classes and, of course, organizing the Main Stationery Cupboard.

"How much chalk do you think you could get your hands on in exchange for three giant jelly snakes?" Minnie pulled the snakes out of her pocket.

"Hmmm," said Tabitha, blowing a bubble with the gum in her mouth. Tabitha was one of those kids who was *always* chewing gum and *never* got caught for it. Tabitha considered the massive jelly snakes that Minnie was dangling in front of her.

"Probably all of the chalk," she said.

"All of the chalk?" repeated Elizabella.

"Yep, I reckon. Mr Crab called the office from the staffroom, there's some sort of tea spillage situation he has to clean up, he won't be back for ages." Tabitha went off to the Main Stationery Cupboard to get the chalk.

A few minutes later, Elizabella and Minnie had assembled a small group of helpers and an enormous amount of chalk, courtesy of Tabitha, who had stuck her gum behind her ear, swapping it for the jelly snakes, which she was now chewing on. She watched Elizabella and Minnie get to work with their helpers.

They were from all years, and had been hand-picked based on Elizabella's confidence that they could draw a straight line. Each kid received a packet of chalk and one piece of paper from Minnie's grid, which represented the part of the playground they were responsible for drawing on.

Soon everyone in the playground had moved to the perimeters so that they weren't stepping where anyone was drawing. They didn't know what was going on, but they were sure it would be good.

Samuel in Reception was the last one drawing. Despite being only five, he drew the straightest lines of anyone at Bilby Creek, and had been given *three* pieces of the grid paper to draw on the ground. He finished drawing his final line and called out: "Done!"

Elizabella and Minnie bustled about the playground, checking everything was in place. When they were satisfied, Elizabella took Minnie by the hand and they walked into the very centre of their **creation.**

"What should we call it?" Elizabella asked.

"How about Humungo Handball?" offered Minnie.

Elizabella nodded. Then she put on her loudest voice as she said, "We declare Humungo Handball open! Everybody grab a square!"

A massive cheer rang through the playground and everyone moved to stand in the squares.

Sandy stood in a square at the very top, took a tennis ball out of his pocket and yelled, "Let the first game of Humungo Handball begin!" He promptly bounced a ball so high and far that it landed about twenty squares diagonally away. And with that, the game took off.

Elizabella and Minnie stood back and admired their work.

"What's this?" asked a familiar voice. It was Mr Gobblefrump. He had been running late for play-ground duty that day because he was busy cleaning up the spilled tea with Mr Crab. While filling his teacup in the staffroom, Mr Gobblefrump had fallen into a daydream about Miss Duck, and before he knew it he'd poured the entire pot of tea on the floor.

"It's called Humungo Handball," said Minnie.

"It's a giant handball court for everyone to play altogether," said Elizabella.

"We drew it with chalk so it will wash off when it rains."

"Which will be tonight, according to the weather forecast."

Mr Gobblefrump took a big, deep breath and looked out over Humungo Handball.

"You've brought everyone together," he said. "And without doing any permanent damage to school property. A marvel, girls."

Minnie and Elizabella looked at each other.

"Pleasure doing business with you," said Minnie.

"Likewise," said Elizabella.

★ ★ ★

Elizabella was leaving school that afternoon with a feeling of satisfaction that she hadn't felt in a long time. Huck ran to catch up with her as she reached the gate.

"Elizabella!" he said. "That was so cool!"

"Thanks, Huck!" she said.

"That's the most fun anyone has had since – since – Pit Pool!"

"What about fishing the toupee off Mr Gobblefrump's head?" asked Elizabella.

"Oh, that was fun," said Huck. "But it was no Pit Pool." Huck smiled at Elizabella.

"Really?" she asked.

"Not to me," said Huck.

"Umm… Huck?"

"Yes?"

Elizabella was about to say something about *like* liking him, but as soon as she started she realized that for the first time since she could remember, she was completely lost for words.

Chapter Eleven

"And this here, you won't believe what this is! It's *none other* than the machine that squirts the toothpaste into the tube! Haven't you always wondered how they do it? Well, this is how!" Mr Gobblefrump explained proudly, pressing the remote to flick to the next photo.

It was evening at Mr Gobblefrump's house and the toothpaste factory slide show had been going for an hour already. "And this one—" He squinted, trying

to make out what it was. "Ah yes, I see that one is a picture of my thumb."

Suddenly he heard an audible snore. It was so loud it gave him a little scare.

"Eep!" he squealed, which woke up Miss Duck.

"Ahhh!" she screamed back, having been frightened awake. She sat upright on the sofa.

"My dear Petunia, did you fall asleep? I would gladly go back any number of slides so that you don't miss a thing!"

"Ah, no!" she said. "No, no, no, no, I remember every moment. It's just sometimes I close my eyes and make a snoring sound when I am *particularly* enjoying myself."

"Splendid," said Mr Gobblefrump, completely satisfied with this response. He clicked the remote again to move on. "And this is a picture of the machine that puts the toothpaste into the box. Can you believe it? There is a machine for *everything* now."

That was it.

"'Scuse me, Chester, nature calls!" Miss Duck promptly stood up, walked to the bathroom and sat on the toilet for five full minutes. And even though she didn't actually go, she was very much relieved.

★ ★ ★

The next day, Miss Duck tried to catch Elizabella's attention before school *and* at both breaktime and lunch, but she couldn't see her little ghostwriter anywhere. Elizabella had spent the day fixated on her Huck Crush – trying to work out what to say to him, and never quite managing to find the words. When the final bell rang for the end of the day, Miss Duck ran out of the tuck shop and finally spotted her.

"Elizabella! Elizabella!"

Elizabella and Huck were about to walk home when they heard a voice ringing through the playground. Elizabella spun around to see Miss Duck peeking out of the tuck shop and gesturing for her to come over. Elizabella suddenly remembered Miss Duck had just been on her date night.

"I'd better go see what that's about," she said, running off.

"I can wait for you if you…" Huck trailed off. She was out of earshot before he could say "like", which he said quietly to himself instead.

When Elizabella got to the tuck shop, Miss Duck was a bit agitated.

"Elizabella, remember how I told you that sometimes you have to humour the people you like?"

"Yes?"

"Maybe I was wrong."

"The toothpaste factory slide show?"

Miss Duck stared into the distance with a look in her eyes like someone who had suffered an unspeakable horror.

"It was … *brutal*," she said. Elizabella's heart sank. If Miss Duck lost interest in Mr Gobblefrump, that would **spell doom** for everyone.

"Don't you need to go out with him again to be sure how you feel?"

"Maybe, I don't know…"

"Come on, Miss Duck, give him one more

chance," Elizabella encouraged.

"Well, he *does* want to take me out to L'Escargots Bilby, the new restaurant in town…"

"That sounds fun!" said Elizabella.

"They serve a fusion of traditional French and Bilby Creek cuisine!" said Miss Duck, getting a little bit excited.

"You've got to go. I'll write you the lovey-est dovey-est poem you've ever seen."

"Maybe you're right. What would I do without you, Elizabella?"

Elizabella felt a twinge of guilt. Of course she cared about Miss Duck's happiness, but that wasn't *really* why she was trying to save the relationship.

Back in the playground, she looked around for her crush, but it seemed Huck had gone home. Minnie, however, was waiting for her. "What happened in there?"

"Bad news, seems like Miss Duck is going cold on Gobblefrump."

"No! This is a disaster of epic proportions," said Minnie.

"I know. They're going out on one more date tomorrow night."

"You'd better write a good poem to reignite their flame."

"Oh, I know, I'm on it," said Elizabella.

"Like Mèng Hàorán good," continued Minnie.

"Who's that?"

Minnie looked at Elizabella, shocked. "You don't know Mèng Hàorán?"

"No, who is that?"

"He's one of *the* most important poets from the Tang Dynasty..."

Elizabella had no idea what Minnie was talking about.

"Ummm ... aka the Golden Age of Chinese poetry?" Minnie said.

Elizabella shrugged. "Nope, no idea."

"I thought you were the poetry expert!" said Minnie. "Let me teach you one of his poems. It's called 'Spring Morning'."

Minnie cleared her throat and began to recite:

"I wake up with the sun up high

Birds chirp everywhere in the sky

Last night a rainstorm passed by

Flowers must have fallen down."

"Wow, what a beautiful poem!" said Elizabella.

"It sounds even better in Mandarin. I'll lend you a book. If you want to be a poetry expert, you need to expand your horizons."

"Seems like I do," agreed Elizabella. "But for now, I have to write **one killer love poem.**"

★ ★ ★

Later in the evening, Elizabella sat at the big old wooden writing table in her room. It was covered in loose paper and notepads and sticky notes. All her walls were, too. Where other kids had band and movie posters or photos of them and their friends, Elizabella's walls were covered in half-finished stories and poems.

She sat with a pen out and a large, pretty sheet of handmade tangerine paper. Pristine. Not a drop of ink on it.

"Think!" Elizabella implored herself, **"Thiiiiiiiiiiink!"** Her brain remained sitting there stubbornly with its arms folded (her brain had arms, made of brains).

"Please, brain!" she said out loud.

I don't wannnnna! said Elizabella's brain sulkily in her head.

"Come on, can't you think of some nice things to say about Mr Gobblefrump?"

No! I can't do it any more!

"Well, what are we going to do?

If you want me to think of nice lovey-dovey things to say, you're going to have to pretend we're writing about someone else.

"Oh..."

And you know who I mean.

Elizabella knew exactly who her brain meant. And an image of a skinny little boy with a lovely smile and sandy hair and a hole in his slime-green shoe and glasses on his eyes and a tennis ball bouncing all over the place came into her head.

She picked up a pen, and started to write...

★ ★ ★

"As you know, electricity powers many of the devices you use every day – light globes, fridges, TVs…"

It was the following morning and Elizabella had given the new poem to a very grateful Miss Duck. Now, in class, Miss Carrol was teaching everyone about electricity, and it had given Elizabella an excellent idea.

"Metal is a very good conductor of electricity," said Miss Carrol. She held up a power cord that had been opened up so you could see what was inside. "That's why the metal wires in this cord are coated in this white plastic, and the bit you touch when you plug the metal prongs into the wall is plastic – otherwise you'd get a shock."

Elizabella decided to share her idea with her new co-conspirator, Minnie. "Hey, Minnie."

"Yes?"

"I have something pretty special planned for lunch. You wanna help me make it happen?"

"Sure!" said Minnie.

"OK, meet me at the silver benches by the big oak tree in the playground."

"See you there, comrade."

Comrade. That's an upgrade from soldier, thought Elizabella, smiling. *Minnie and I can be comrades.*

★ ★ ★

At lunchtime, Elizabella was standing next to a set of silver benches in the playground. On the ground in front of her was a single square of carpet. All the carpet in the school was made up of individual squares, and sometimes they came loose. Elizabella had been eyeing a piece of it in the library that had completely come away and sat there, unstuck, near the History of Concrete section that nobody ever borrowed from. She knew it would come in handy someday. And that day was today.

Elizabella and her set-up were cordoned off by an elaborate tent-like barricade made from large twigs, rubbish bins, discarded school jumpers and painting smocks from the art room. Students were beginning to queue up to see what Elizabella was up to. Everything was going perfectly except that Comrade Minnie had never shown up. So instead, Elizabella had enlisted Sandy to help her. He was acting as her salesman, standing just outside the barricade, gathering customers. Elizabella had given him some catchy rhymes to say, to lure in customers.

"Step right up! Over this way! The Electric Woman will make your day!"

Of course her gang were the first in the queue. Huck, Ava and Evie had been wondering why Elizabella wasn't around to play handball – and they were keen to see what she had cooked up.

Huck was the first inside, where he saw that Elizabella had tied a jumper around her head and was standing on the little square of carpet stomping and scuffing her feet on it over and over again.

"Are you ready to feel the power of the Electric Woman?" asked Elizabella, a little out of breath.

"Yes!" said Huck.

"Then sit yourself down on this magical silver

bench," she said, gesturing to the seat.

Huck sat down, and Elizabella upped her speed, really rubbing her shoes hard on the little square of carpet. Huck had no idea what was going on. Suddenly, Elizabella stopped and leaned down. She touched Huck on the shoulder and...

ZAAAP!

"Eeeek!" he squealed. When she touched him, she had given him a **giant shock** of static electricity.

"She really is electric!" Huck said, running out of the tent.

Excellent, thought Elizabella, knowing that a positive testimonial from someone you know is the most powerful marketing tool of all – and basically everyone in the playground knew Huck.

The word spread and people began forming a long queue. Elizabella rubbed her feet on the little square of carpet and gave electric shocks to everyone who came in. But, after about ten minutes, the queue started to thin, and then disappeared altogether.

Eventually Sandy came in.

"What's going on out there?" Elizabella asked.

"Ahhh, I don't know. Everyone has gathered right down the other end of the playground," said Sandy. He took his job seriously, and didn't want to desert Elizabella. But, as he bounced from foot to foot, Elizabella could tell he was desperate to see what all the fuss was about. She sighed.

"You'd better go and check it out," she said, forcing a smile.

"Thank you!" Sandy replied and, with the relief of someone who has just spotted a water fountain in the middle of the desert, he ran for it.

Elizabella peeked out of the tent. Everyone was laughing and cheering and looking at something big and round. Elizabella squinted to try to make it out. It was a giant exercise ball ... wearing trousers?

Reluctantly, she walked over to inspect further. Minnie had made a life-size sculpture of Mr Gobblefrump. Elizabella gathered from the squeals of excitement that Minnie had gone to Mr Gobblefrump's locker and taken a spare pair of his trousers, then dressed the exercise ball in them. Then

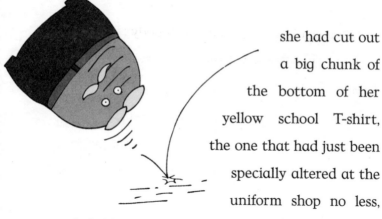

she had cut out a big chunk of the bottom of her yellow school T-shirt, the one that had just been specially altered at the uniform shop no less, and she'd torn it into strips to make a moustache and toupee. Then she'd stuck on a set of googly eyes and put three bottles of orange juice next to him.

Elizabella was upset. *If Minnie really was a good friend, wouldn't she have come to help me with my plan, just like I did with Humungo Handball, instead of stealing my thunder?*

Elizabella wondered how Mr Gobblefrump was going to take it. *Probably not well,* she thought. Minnie had stolen his trousers, after all. Then she heard that sound from yesterday coming through the thick crowd of kids. "Huh! Huh! Huh!"

Mr Gobblefrump emerged and stood next to his likeness, *laughing.* "Hee hee hee!" he cried out, "Minnie! You are a true artiste!"

"Minnie! Minnie! Minnie!" everybody chanted.

Well, thought Elizabella. *This really takes the biscuit.*

Chapter Twelve

"I'm sorry," said Minnie in class that afternoon. "You know what it's like. Sometimes you see an opportunity and you have to take it. And when I saw Mr Gobblefrump's open locker with the trousers falling out, I just had to."

Elizabella gathered this was Minnie's attempt at an apology, but she didn't think it was a very good one and even if it was, she wasn't ready to accept it. Not only had Minnie *abandoned* Elizabella when she said she'd help her, she had also completely stolen Elizabella's spotlight. So instead of responding to Minnie, Elizabella hunched her shoulders and lowered her head and made herself into a tight little silent ball of anger.

After school, she wandered around the playground looking for Huck. She wanted to walk home with him and unload about her Minnie-troubles.

Eventually she found him down by Pit Pool, which had been completely transformed back into a boring empty sandpit, as though Elizabella's legendary aqua creation had never existed at all. He was sitting in it with Ava, Evie and ... Minnie!

"Hey, Huck, you ready to walk home?" Elizabella asked.

"Actually, I'm going to go to the park with Minnie," said Huck, a little quietly, as though he knew this was some sort of betrayal.

"Same," said Ava and Evie, also quietly.

"Elizabella, you should come with us!" said Huck hopefully. Elizabella looked at her friends.

"Come on, Elizabella," said Minnie. "We're going to go to the park to see if we can teach all the dogs there different names to confuse them and their owners."

"That's … mean," said Elizabella.

"Just joking," said Minnie. "I'm not *evil*."

Elizabella wondered how many times a non-evil person had to protest that they weren't evil.

"Yeah, Elizabella," said Ava. "We're not *evil*."

We, thought Elizabella. *They're a "we" now*. It seemed like *all* of Elizabella's best friends had become **Minnie followers.**

"I think I'll just go home," said Elizabella.

As she walked out of the school, she saw Mr Gobblefrump at the gates cheerily saying goodbye to everyone. And every time he'd bid a kid farewell, he'd proudly take off his toupee and bow, then put it back on his head, like an old-fashioned man tipping his hat.

"Goodbye, Irma! Au revoir, Little Samuel! Cheerio, Elizabella!"

Elizabella didn't think she'd ever seen such a

happy man. And *she* had helped to make him that way. She had made him *proud* of his toupee! *Everyone* was happy.

So why wasn't Elizabella happy too?

* * *

"The thing is," Larry croaked in Lizish, "I think Minnie actually likes you, quite a bit. And even if you don't always see eye to eye, that doesn't mean you can't be friends, possibly even learn from each other. Think of how many people think *you* cross the line with your pranks, even though you try not to hurt people and make up for it with Sorry Poems. Oh, and you must try to separate your feelings for Huck from the Minnie situation. Just because Huck thinks Minnie is cool, doesn't mean he likes you any less. Don't forget, you and Huck have a very old friendship, going all the way back to nursery. Minnie's been around for five minutes. And if you really *like* like Huck, then the Elizabella I know wouldn't sit around and worry about anyone else, she'd go out and do something about it!"

"Why did I waste my time telling all my problems to a lizard?" said Elizabella, exasperated. "If only you could actually talk instead of croak, I bet you'd have some really interesting things to say." She patted Larry on the head.

"Oh, you have *got* to be kidding me!" croaked Larry. He had just spent a solid ten minutes giving Elizabella frankly excellent advice (in his humble opinion) about her situation, and it seemed she hadn't understood a single word. **Being a lizard was rough.**

Elizabella went to the freezer and pulled out a blue ice pop.

"I may as well ask this ice pop what to do about my situation." She continued, speaking seriously to the ice pop: "Oh, Mrs Ice Pop, please fix all my problems for me."

"Pffft!" croaked Larry. "An *ice pop*? What a ridiculous notion! An ice pop isn't sentient! It doesn't have thoughts or feelings!" He caught what he was saying. "Then again, people don't seem to understand that *I* am a conscious being with thoughts and feelings and ideas and a yearning to learn ... perhaps this ice pop has emotions too?" He stared at the ice pop in Elizabella's hands and concentrated really hard on it.

"Thank you," he thought he may have heard the ice pop say in Iceish. Although it could have just been the sound of the ice crushing in Elizabella's mouth! Was Mrs Ice Pop dead?

"Larry, are you OK?" Elizabella had noticed Larry was staring at her with one eye flickering. If she didn't know any better, she'd say he looked like he was in shock.

"I think Larry needs some food," said Elizabella to Toddberry, who had been sitting at the dining room table puzzling over something tricky in *Fierce Frogs IV*.

Larry let out a loud croak in protest, one of the loudest they'd ever heard him make. Of course they misinterpreted this as enthusiastic agreement that food was in order. But Larry couldn't eat anything right now!

Toddberry went to the fridge and pulled out a big iceberg lettuce. Larry watched as he pulled off five giant leaves, one at a time. With each leaf removal, Larry's eyes twitched and he let out a massive croak, imagining the possibility that each leaf could have feelings.

"He must be *really* hungry," said Toddberry.

★ ★ ★

A little while later, Elizabella walked to the park. She scuffed her shoes deep into the dirt and played with her giant hair knot even more than usual. She wasn't sure why exactly, but she'd had a sudden urge to go there after unloading to Larry. After all, the park didn't belong to anybody, there was no reason she couldn't go even though she had told her friends she was just going to spend the afternoon at home. And if they happened to be there with Minnie and she happened to join them in whatever they were doing and she *happened* to have a good time in the process, **well so be it.**

Elizabella arrived at the park to find Ava, Evie and Huck up the top of the slippery dip.

"Elizabella!" cried Huck, seeing her coming towards them. "You just missed Minnie!"

"Oh, that's a shame," said Elizabella, while really trying to feel like it was a shame, even though she didn't feel like that at all.

"What did you guys get up to?" she yelled up to them from the bottom of the slippery dip. "Did you teach the dogs to sing 'Baa Baa Black Sheep'? Did you find a magical universe in the golden wattle tree ruled by a giant lady flea? Did you dig a tunnel under the roundabout all the way to the zoo and then dig holes up into the animals' cages so that the animals could secretly come out of their cages at night and scurry and stomp and fly through the tunnel and come and play in the park without any of the zookeepers or any of the adults in Bilby Creek ever knowing about it?"

The three of them stared at her, blinking.

"No," said Ava, "but that's a *great* idea."

Elizabella thought about it. It *was* a great idea. She filed it away for a rainy day. *Although not actually for a rainy day*, she thought. *It would be hard enough to pull off as it is, let alone if it was raining.*

"We just played on the equipment for a bit," said Evie.

"Oh … right," said Elizabella. "And what else?"

Huck shrugged. "We talked about the homework Miss Carrol gave us for a while."

"That sounds … nice?" said Elizabella.

"Yeah, it was fine," said Evie. "What are we going to do now?"

Elizabella thought about it for a second. "We haven't raced the seesaws!" she said.

She ran over to the seesaws and plonked down on one of them, and her friends slid down the slippery dip to join her.

"Hurry up! They're about to fire the starting pistol!"

★ ★ ★

Miss Duck sat opposite Mr Gobblefrump. She had put on a nice frock, slapped on some make-up and had the fresh poem tucked into her pocket. She was ready to give dating Mr Gobblefrump **one last shot.** She was reading through the menu at L'Escargots Bilby – it certainly looked intriguing.

Bouillabaisse à la Creek: a tomato, herb and seafood stew, made with the catch of the day (ask your waiter for details).

Croque Monsieur et Pavlova: French fried ham and cheese sandwich with a side of Bilby Creek pavlova.

Miss Duck was intrigued … if a little sceptical.

The waiter came over to take their order.

"I'll have the Bœuf Bourguignon Bilby Creek Sausage Roll," said Mr Gobblefrump.

"And I'll have the, ummm, Bouillabaisse à la Creek?" said Miss Duck, uncertainly.

"Excellent choice, Madame," said the waiter. "Today's catch is a lobster and a packet of salt and vinegar crisps that came up with it in the fishing net." The waiter put his fingers to his lips and made a kissing sound, as if to say *Delicious!*

"Oh dear..." said Miss Duck as the waiter flounced off to the kitchen.

"So, Petunia," said Mr Gobblefrump, "after the great success of last time, I thought perhaps next week I might show you the slide show of my trip to the Bilby Creek Slug-quarium. You wouldn't believe the slight variations in brownish grey that these slugs come in, but they are numerous, my dear, I assure you!"

And with that Miss Duck realized she had every answer she was looking for when it came to the future of herself and Mr Gobblefrump.

"Chester," she said, putting a hand on his. "We need to talk..."

"Oh..." said Mr Gobblefrump.

"I think maybe we should just be ... good friends."

He paused a moment. Then put on the bravest face he could muster and raised his glass.

"To good friends."

★ ★ ★

Elizabella was back at home. The family had eaten dinner and now she and Toddberry were sitting in the lounge watching cartoons. Larry the Lizard had eventually calmed down and devoured the lettuce. He may not have known for *certain* whether or not the lettuce had feelings, but he could confidently say it was delicious. And in the end, yumminess had won the day.

"Elizabella," said Toddberry, "have you thought about trying to be friends with Minnie? I mean, you guys seem to have a lot in common."

Elizabella and Larry both turned to Toddberry, amazed.

"And if you have a crush on Huck," Toddberry continued, "then, well, maybe you should stop whining and go and tell him about it. That's what the Elizabella I know would do."

Oh my god ... that boy is stealing my material! thought Larry. *Does this mean he can understand me and is pretending not to?*

"Hey, Toddberry! Can you hear me? I *know* you can hear me!" croaked Larry at Toddberry.

"You can't possibly be hungry again?" said Toddberry to Larry.

"Wow, Toddberry!" said Elizabella. "That's actually really great advice. Thanks a bunch!"

She leaned over and gave her brother a hug.

"Well, what are big brothers for?" he asked.

"Honestly, I had no idea until right now."

"I can't believe this!" croaked Larry. "This is stupendously unfair!"

Toddberry looked at the lizard. "Elizabella, I think Larry is trying to give you some advice too!"

Elizabella laughed. "Naaaw, thanks, Larry."

Toddberry picked up Larry and held him out to Elizabella, then put on a croaky voice and said, "My advice is to eat loads of lettuce and then do a poo in the garden. That always makes me feel better!"

"Oh, that's great advice, Larry!" said Elizabella. "I'll be sure to give that a go!"

"Don't you put those silly words in my mouth!" croaked Larry. "I will not be patronized!"

Toddberry pulled the rubber lid off their dad's reusable coffee cup, which was sitting on the table in front of them. He put it on Larry's head.

"Look at me! My name is Larry and I have a special hat!"

Elizabella and Toddberry laughed.

How demeaning, thought Larry.

Elizabella stood up. "I'm going to go make us each an Ice Cream Fort." This was Toddberry's favourite dessert. Or rather, the only thing Elizabella cooked that he actually liked. It was whatever ice cream they had in the freezer put in a bowl with loads of whatever biscuits they had in the cupboard stuck around the edges. She skipped out of the room.

And as she did, Toddberry stared straight into Larry's lizard eyes and winked.

Chapter Thirteen

It was the evening everyone had been waiting for all term – the Bilby Creek Fête. Fairy lights, baubles, bells, tinsel and streamers festooned the place, swinging from tree to tree to fence to pillar to post, creating a glorious rainbow canopy that shone and glittered in the moonlight. Elizabella and Minnie had made some big alterations to the playground that term, but even they would agree that this was pretty amazing. If they were speaking to each other, that is.

At the arm-wrestling table sat Miss Carrol, the undefeated champion, waiting for a new rival. Mr Biffington was in a beautiful purple and golden tent reading people's fortunes. And in the middle of the playground was a giant inflatable wombat-shaped bouncy castle, which Mr Crab stood by, supervising.

Miss Duck, who was wearing a special gold-sequinned apron, had set up a giant feast on a long chequered table. There was pea soup, chicken pies, cucumber sandwiches and sausage rolls. There were Black Forest and Madeira cakes, crumpets and toffee apples, and marshmallows for roasting on a little fire.

Elizabella and Huck entered the fête carrying a big regular bread house. They had had an extremely fun afternoon making it. So much so that Elizabella had forgotten all about Minnie. She had the genius idea of making the house out of Extreme Fairy Bread, which had the natural adhesive of strawberry jam and the natural prettiness of sprinkles. Huck had thought to toast the bread first so that it was firmer and more structurally sound. They'd both decided *not* to set it on fire because they didn't want to go to jail. It was hard to deny it – they made a great team.

They saw Ava and Evie when they arrived.

"What's that?" asked Ava, pointing to the strange, edible sculpture.

"It's a regular bread house!" said Huck proudly.

"Cool!" said Evie.

Elizabella looked at Huck and smiled.

They saw some commotion at the arm wrestling table, then a big cheer went up. They all ran over to see what had happened.

An announcement blared: "And the winner, who has managed to best our hitherto undefeated champion Miss Carrol … is …. Minnie!"

Everyone cheered.

"Minnie, you have won this two-hundred-piece set of Pickles Pencils!"

Minnie took the prize and did a massive bow. She came over and joined the others. Elizabella braced herself. She was having a good time and hardly in the mood for Minnie.

"Cool, huh?" said Minnie, showing everyone her prize.

Daphne came skipping over to them, chewing on a candy necklace.

"Wow!" she said. "That's the biggest set of Pickles Pencils I have *ever* seen!"

Minnie considered it for a minute, then handed it to Daphne. "You can have it," she said.

Daphne stared at her, her mouth forming an **"O"** that got wider and wider, like a sinkhole opening up the earth, until it looked like her whole face was one gaping wide mouth with some tiny features squished at the top.

"That's the nicest thing … *ever*!" she spluttered out and gave Minnie a big kiss on the cheek before running away. Elizabella was shocked.

"Wow, Minnie," said Elizabella. "That *was* nice."

"Yeah, well," said Minnie, who had actually surprised herself.

"I'll be back in a minute, guys," said Elizabella. She went over to visit Miss Duck and gave her the bread house to sell.

"What a beautiful regular bread house!" said Miss Duck.

"You've heard of them?" asked Elizabella.

"Oh, yes. They're a delicacy!"

Maybe Mum was a better cook than everyone gave her credit for? Elizabella wondered.

"So, how was the date?" she asked.

"I really tried, truly I did," said Miss Duck. "But the Slug-quarium?"

"I like the Slug-quarium!" said Elizabella.

"Yes, dear, but would you ever ask somebody to watch a several-hours-long slide show of pictures of you at the slug-quarium?"

"No, I would never do that to someone I liked," said Elizabella truthfully.

"Though it was fun while it lasted, the Gobblefrump–Duck dalliance has come to an end. And I want you to take this back." Miss Duck reached into her pocket and pulled out the last poem Elizabella had given her.

"It really is the most beautiful poem that I have ever read," said Miss Duck. "You should give it to someone special one day."

Elizabella smiled and stuffed the poem into her

pocket. "Thanks, Miss Duck."

The sound of a big commotion came from the other side of the playground.

Minnie! thought Elizabella. She knew that Minnie *must* have a big scheme planned for the fête.

Minnie marched up and down the length of the playground. She had assembled twenty kids into two lines. Each line of ten kids had tied their shoelaces together.

"OK, it's time for the eleven-legged race!" she said. "Three ... two..."

Mr Gobblefrump appeared.

Oh no! thought Elizabella. *Now that Mr Gobblefrump is heartbroken, when he realizes what Minnie has done, **he's gonna lose it!***

"No, Minnie!" said Elizabella helplessly from her side of the playground. Even though she and Minnie had their major differences, she didn't want her to get in trouble.

"One!"

The race began. And as twenty kids awkwardly half-walked, half-ran down the playground tied together, Elizabella closed her eyes and saw the eleven-legged race unfurl in her mind. Firstly, Ava would trip over a stick and sprain her ankle. As she cried out in pain she would knock over Sandy, whose knee would connect with an acorn and start pouring blood. All the way down the line the kids would fall like dominoes, until they fell right onto the other line of kids. Suddenly, everyone would be on the ground. The last kid to go down would be Huck, whose glasses would fall off right onto the bouncy castle and the moon would shine through them, creating a laser beam that would burn a hole in the bouncy castle, and the whole thing would deflate, swallowing everyone inside, and then the police would come and arrest everyone who was still alive.

Elizabella waited for the inevitable scream of Mr Gobblefrump.

"And the winner is..."

She opened her eyes. Mr Gobblefrump was announcing the winner. And he was ... smiling? It had gone off without a hitch.

"Unclear!" said Mr Gobblefrump with a laugh. "Great game, Minnie!"

Elizabella was so confused. Even though no one had died, the eleven-legged race clearly violated at least seventeen Bilby Creek Primary School rules that she knew of. Surely Mr Gobblefrump would be angrier than ever?

Miss Duck, who had watched the race with Elizabella, saw her confusion at Mr Gobblefrump's response. "You know, Elizabella, sometimes even *Mr Gobblefrump* just likes to have fun."

Elizabella looked at all the kids who had raced trying to untangle themselves from one another and Mr Gobblefrump with them, laughing away.

Elizabella took advantage of not being tied up and headed off to think about what Miss Duck had said.

★ ★ ★

Huck found Elizabella a little dazed and confused.

"That eleven-legged race was something else, wasn't it?" he said.

"Yes, ah, something else," she replied distractedly.

"There are some kids eating the regular bread house. Cool, huh?"

"Yes … umm … cool," she said.

"Hey, look, there's a unicorn over there with bees for eyes and a giant ice cream cone for a horn and because the cone is upside-down, ice cream is dripping all over its face and all over the bees," said Huck.

"Yes … unicorn," said Elizabella.

Huck stopped walking. "OK, Elizabella, spill."

"Hmm?"

"Clearly something is on your mind. What is it?"

Elizabella stopped walking too. She turned to her friend. "Oh, Huck…"

"Elizabella, I'm your best friend. Tell me, what's going on?"

And Elizabella just couldn't hold it in any more. She started to story-vomit – and once she'd started spilling her guts, she just couldn't stop until everything she'd been holding in had come out.

Well … *almost* everything.

Huck was stunned. He sat down. He was trying to take it all in.

"Wow," he said eventually. "I can't believe you've been keeping an epic teacher romance poetry scheme a secret this whole time!"

"Neither can I!" said Elizabella. She sat down next to Huck.

"You know you can always tell me anything," he said, and put an arm around her shoulder.

"Thanks, Huck."

Elizabella had a sudden urge. She reached into her pocket and pulled out the poem.

"Here," she said, thrusting it into Huck's hand.

"What's this?" he asked.

"It's nothing," she said, snatching it back.

Elizabella, what are you doing? Stop! Being! A! Coward!

"Shut up, brain!" said Elizabella out loud.

Huck just sat there, a bit confused.

"Just joking, it's for you," she said, slowly giving

him back the poem. Huck went to open it.

"No! Don't open it!"

"Well, what should I do with it?" he said.

"Open it!"

Huck went to open it again.

"Not now! Later! When I'm gone!"

Huck put the poem in his pocket.

Then Elizabella ran far, far away.

Once she had disappeared into the distance, Huck pulled the poem out of his pocket, opened it and began to read…

I *like* like your eyes
I *like* like your hair
I *like* like your glasses
Through which you stare
I *like* like that you're kind and you understand me
And when I feel sad you're who I want to see
I *like* like your smile and the hole in your shoe
But most most of all, I *like* like you

Huck looked up to the sky and smiled as his whole body started to go golden warm from the tips of his toes to his head, like an empty jar filling up with honey.

Chapter Fourteen

Elizabella ran and ran and ran through the fête until she ran straight into her dad.

"Elizabella!" he said.

She sniffed the air. Something was strange. "Dad, are you wearing cologne?"

"Darling, I need to tell you something." He took her by the hand and walked her to one of the silver benches in the school. Toddberry was sitting there already. He was eating a toffee apple by shoving it between his hair curtains into where his mouth presumably was.

"Elizabella, I've wanted to tell you this for a while, but you may find it a little bit upsetting," said Martin.

"What is it, Dad?"

"The thing is … I'm here on a – a—"

"Date," offered Toddberry. "Dad's on a date."

Elizabella flung her arms around her dad. "Dad, that's wonderful!"

"Oh!" said Martin, a little taken aback.

"I'm so happy!" said Elizabella. And she really meant it. Her dad hadn't been on a date since her mum died and he really deserved to go out and have some fun.

"You won't be so happy when you find out who it's with," said Toddberry.

"What, it's not Miss Duck, is it?"

"Darling," said Martin, "I'm on a date with … Leanne."

Elizabella was confused. "Leanne? But the only Leanne I know is…"

"That's right," said Toddberry. "Huck's mum."

Elizabella froze, her eyes wide as cupcakes.

Suddenly, from the other side of the playground, she heard a giant:

"NNNNNN OOO OOO OOOOOOO OOOO O!!!!!!"

It was Huck. He was standing there, staring at his mum.

Elizabella joined in on the scream.

"NNNNN OOOO OO OOOOOO OO OOO OOOO O OO OO!!!!!!"

And their collective scream rang out over Bilby Creek.

★ ★ ★

Elizabella was walking around the fête anxiously. She had been avoiding everyone. Her dad, Toddberry, her friends, anyone who wanted to know why she screamed and, most of all, Huck. A million thoughts were running through her head. So much so that she didn't notice she'd run into Minnie until she'd bounced right off her.

"Elizabella!" said Minnie. "Did you see the eleven-legged race?"

"How could I have missed it?" asked Elizabella. "I thought you were going to be in all the trouble in the universe because Miss Duck broke it off with Mr Gobblefrump, but apparently he's still happy."

"Well, that's a relief," said Minnie. "Because I'm just getting started."

Elizabella stared at her. "Do you *ever* get in trouble? Like *ever*?"

Minnie shrugged. Then she skipped off towards the library.

Elizabella saw Huck standing just a few metres away. He was clearly avoiding her as much as she was avoiding him. But the playground was only so big and they'd have to deal with each other eventually. Elizabella bit the bullet and walked over to him.

They had a lot to talk about. It was extremely awkward.

"That poem," began Huck.

"Oh, yeah, don't worry about it," said Elizabella.

"OK," said Huck.

They walked along in silence for a little while.

"Actually," said Huck, "I just want you to know that before we were practically brother and sister, I read your poem and I liked it. Like *like* liked it."

Elizabella smiled, then her smile fell away. "Boo," she said. "It's our parents."

Martin and Leanne were sharing candyfloss. They spotted their respective children.

"How's it going, kids?" asked Leanne. She turned to Elizabella. "I just won this monkey for your dad in that silly squirting-clowns-in-the-mouth game!" Elizabella mustered a smile. "Maybe he'll let you have it?" said Leanne, handing her a giant monkey plush toy. Then she looked at her own son, who seemed a little sad.

"Sorry, Huck," said Martin. "I'm sure your mum can win you one too, she's very good."

"I know she is," said Huck with a tiny smile.

"Dad," blurted out Elizabella, "are me and Huck going to have to be brother and sister now?"

Leanne and Martin started laughing.

"What?" said Huck. "Are we?!"

"Kids, kids," said Martin. "We've been on *one* date before tonight."

"To a ridiculous action film," added Leanne. "Not even a romantic one!"

Oh, thought Elizabella, *that's where Dad went in such a hurry the day of the Pit Pool incident! No wonder he didn't want to tell me.*

"We have no idea what's going to happen," said Martin. "But as far as you two becoming siblings? Well, *if* anything like that was going to happen – which is the biggest *if* in the world – then we're talking ages away."

"Like years," said Leanne.

"Maybe decades," said Martin.

Elizabella and Huck glanced at each other. The two of them had barely been *alive* for a decade, so if they were *ever* going to be brother and sister, that was a lifetime away.

Elizabella smiled to herself.

"Hey, what's going on over at the monkey bars?" asked Leanne. Everyone turned around to see Minnie walking over towards them, dragging beanbags from the library behind her. When she got to the monkey bars she threw them on top, where they joined several other beanbags that were already there.

While everyone had been busy eating and playing and having a good time, Minnie had taken advantage of the other distractions to sneak into the library and pull out all the beanbags. She'd also gone to the caretaker's cupboard and found a leaf blower. She'd put the blower and the beanbags on top of the monkey bars and was now climbing them.

By now everyone at the fête had realized something was going on and they were all looking at her. A giant grin came across her face. She unzipped one of the beanbags, revved up the leaf blower and blew white beans high into the sky, which then rained down on the playground, coating it in a layer of...

"SNOW!!!!!" everyone cried as they ran and skipped

and played in the little white beany snow droplets.

"IT'S SNOWING IN BILBY CREEK!"

As the bean snow mingled with the baubles and tinsel and all the decorations and thickened on the ground, magic filled the air. Elizabella looked around at everyone. Miss Duck collected the bean snowflakes from her hair, put them in her hands and then blew them away. Then she jumped about as they fell back down on her head. Ava and Evie were synchronized skiing in their plimsolls from one end of the playground to the other, while Sandy spun around in circles like an ice skater. Elizabella saw her dad dancing with Leanne in the snow. He gave her a big dip like in the movies. Even Toddberry was holding the hair curtains away from his head, and his eyes were as wide as pies as he took in the sight.

Minnie descended the monkey bars and walked through the playground watching everyone play. She was glad to have made everyone so happy. And there was just one person she wanted to talk to about it.

"So?" said Minnie, bounding up to Elizabella. "What do you think?"

Elizabella couldn't hide how impressed she was. And she didn't even really want to.

"Minnie, it's amazing. You've made the whole of Bilby Creek happy. And the logistics alone... How long have you been planning this?"

"Since you told me you'd never seen snow before," said Minnie, smiling.

Elizabella stared. "But that was on your first day!"

"Yep. I could tell you were cool from when I first met you. And I wanted to do something nice for you."

Elizabella couldn't believe it. "You did all this ... for me?" she asked.

"Yep," said Minnie.

The girls smiled at each other.

"Well, you and Mr Gobblefrump," said Minnie, gesturing towards the middle of the playground where Mr Gobblefrump was on the ground rolling about in the snow.

"He looks like the happiest puppy in the world," said Elizabella.

"Yeah," said Minnie. "Who needs romance when you have a playground full of beanbag snow to play with?" And with that she lay down on the ground and started moving her arms and legs out from side to side. "Come and make snow angels with me!"

Elizabella giggled and lay down next to her friend. They both moved their arms and legs from side to side, making snow angels on the ground and laughing and cracking jokes as the moon shone down on the first and last ever snowy summer night in Bilby Creek.

NAME Elizamamabella

SUBJECT Fixytales

YEAR Since For Ever

The Princess and The Pea
or Nobody Likes a Whinger

~~~~~~

A Fixytale by Elizamamabella

Once upon a time in a world without internet dating, a prince – let's call him Barry – was having difficulty finding true love. Even though there were *plenty* of funny, intelligent and attractive women in his kingdom, he hadn't quite found that certain *va-va-voom* with any of them.

It was a stormy morning, one where the sky made all sorts of strange sounds and it was so dark it could have been night-time. Prince Barry was sitting at one end of his extra-long and fancy dining table eating breakfast. His mum (the Queen), who he lived with, was sitting down the other end. They always sat like this, even though it made it very hard to have a conversation.

"Will you pass the salt, Barry?" asked the Queen.

"What?" shouted Barry.

"I SAID, WILL YOU PASS THE SALT?" she screamed back.

"NO, I DIDN'T SEE A THUNDERBOLT," he shouted back, looking out the window.

"Oh, forget it," said the Queen.

"WHAT?" Barry shouted again.

"I said you're a grown man and it's high time you found someone and moved out of my house!" the Queen said, taking advantage of the fact that Barry couldn't hear her to get something off her chest. But Barry had just cleaned his ear with a napkin, which, although gross, had gone a long way to improving his hearing.

"I heard that, Mama," he said.

There was a sound at the door. It was the extremely obnoxious doorbell they'd just had installed, which played the "Happy Birthday" tune. It was the Queen's idea.

"I know it won't make sense ninety-nine

per cent of the time, but imagine how happy it will make people who come to the door when it really *is* their birthday," she'd explained to Barry when she'd had it installed.

Now who could be visiting? They certainly weren't expecting anyone…

Barry got up and threw open the door.

There, standing completely sodden on the doorstep, was a woman.

Barry stared at her. Her shoes were untied and her stockings were laddered. Her hair had a mind of its own, and roamed wet and curly all over the place.

She is … The One! Barry thought.

"Are you going to just stand there and stare or are you going to let me in? It's wet out here!" said the woman.

"I'm so sorry!" said Barry, embarrassed. "Allow me to introduce myself, I'm Barry, Prince of—"

"Yeah, yeah," said the woman, letting herself into the castle.

"And you're...?"

"Sheila. Princess Sheila." She grabbed a curtain and started drying herself off. "Nice grub!" she said, looking at the table that was sagging under the weight of loads of fancy things with unpronounceable names.

"Please," said the Queen, "tuck in."

Now perhaps it had something to do with how badly the Queen wanted to have her giant castle to herself, but she saw some special qualities in this unexpected visitor.

After Princess Sheila made her way through ten croissants, eleven pieces of toast and a fistful of ham, she popped one final berry into her mouth and sighed. "I'm pooped!"

"Of course," said the Queen. She bustled into one of the three thousand guestrooms in the house and started assembling an extra special bed for Princess Sheila.

Meanwhile, Barry and Sheila chatted.

"So, Barry, what's your favourite animal?"

"The house mouse!"

"Well, that's *boring*."

"I'm sorry."

Luckily the Queen didn't take too long, as the conversation wasn't exactly flowing. "Your boudoir awaits," the Queen exclaimed, and led her guest into the newly prepared room.

"Crikey!" Princess Sheila said, craning her neck up in an attempt to see the top of the bed. "There must be twenty mattresses there!"

"There are," the Queen said. "I'll leave you to your slumber now." She drew the doors closed behind her.

Several hours passed. Barry did some French knitting in one of the castle's eighty-three parlours, while the Queen attempted to teach herself how to sing and play "What Makes You Beautiful" by One Direction on the piano. How unfortunate, Prince Barry reflected, that of all the eighty-three parlours at their disposal, they had both chosen the same one for their respective afternoon activities.

Suddenly, the doors to the parlour flung open.

Princess Sheila stood there, looking incredibly underslept.

"My dear!" said the Queen. "Is everything all right?"

"It's not!" said Princess Sheila. "That bed is *rotten!*"

The Queen gasped, injured by this remark.

"I haven't slept a wink!" Princess Sheila continued. "There was something very hard pressing into my back. After tossing and turning *for ever*, I climbed down, shoved my hand right under the bottom mattress and found ... *this!*"

Princess Sheila produced a single pea.

"And I know why you put it there!"

The Queen and Barry looked at Princess Sheila, confused.

"What are you on about, dear?" said the Queen.

"Clearly you wanted to see if I was *sensitive* enough to be a real princess, thus making me an eligible bachelorette for Prince Barry.

So you placed this solitary pea under twenty mattresses to see if I could feel it! And I have proven myself!"

"No," said the Queen, "I just tried to make you a nice tall bed for the ultimate dozing bliss, but I see now my efforts were in vain." The Queen looked sad.

"Well, what's the deal with this pea, then?" asked Princess Sheila.

"I don't know!" said the Queen. "It's a big house to clean, I must have missed that pea."

"Oh … right," said Princess Sheila.

Prince Barry had thought Princess Sheila was The One, but could he really marry someone who would make such a fuss about a pea under *twenty* mattresses?

Princess Sheila turned to Barry. "So, we getting married or what?"

Barry thought about this. Maybe the pea situation was a warning – could she be like this all the time? Or perhaps it was just a one-off… At this point it was impossible to know.

"I think we should go on a few dates first," he concluded.

Princess Sheila shrugged. "Makes sense, we've only known each other for like three hours and I was trying to sleep for two of them."

With that, Prince Barry called Princess Sheila a Horse-Uber and she went off into the day.

And the Prince and Princess decided to date for at least a year before making any drastic decisions about the rest of their lives.

The End

Acknowledgements

To Mama and Dad for thinking we could do anything and to Mark and Sam for exactly the same.

And Maja and Ned, you kids are all right.

And to our Rufus, of course.

Filakia, we love you.

THE ILLUSTRATOR

THE AUTHOR

About the Author

ZOË NORTON LODGE is a writer, actress and television presenter, known for her work on ABC TV's *The Checkout* and the live storytelling night and podcast *Story Club*, as well as her collected short stories *Almost Sincerely*. *Elizabella Meets Her Match* is her debut children's novel.

About the Illustrator

By day, GEORGIA NORTON LODGE leads her branding team at a Sydney-based design agency. By night, she moonlights as an illustrator with her side project Georgia Draws a House, where she delights people with deliveries of their hand-drawn homes. She's also Zoë's younger sister. This is their second book together.

"Delightful and moving"
M. G. Leonard, author of *Beetle Boy*

Astrid Glimmerdal loves to spend her days
racing down the mountainside on her sledge and
skis – the faster the better! She just wishes there
were other children to share her adventures. She
is thrilled when a new family comes to stay,
but things don't get off to a good start. Then
Astrid discovers that Gunnvald, her grumpy best
friend, has been keeping a big secret from her.

Everything is changing in Astrid's world and she's
not happy about it. Luckily, she has a plan...